Dr. Nikola's Experiment

Guy Boothby

CONTENTS

CHAPTER I. TIRED OF LIFE
CHAPTER II. A NEW IMPETUS
CHAPTER III. THE MYSTERIOUS CHINAMAN
CHAPTER IV. THE CHINAMAN'S ESCAPE
CHAPTER V. ALLERDEYNE CASTLE
CHAPTER VI. LIFE IN THE CASTLE
CHAPTER VII. LOVE REIGNS
CHAPTER VIII. THE RESULT OF THE EXPERIMENT
CHAPTER IX. WAR AND PEACE

Dr. Nikola's Experiment

CHAPTER I. TIRED OF LIFE

IT is sad enough at any time for a man to be compelled to confess himself a failure, but I think it will be admitted that it is doubly so at that period of his career when he is still young enough to have some flickering sparks of ambition left, while he is old enough to be able to appreciate at their proper value the overwhelming odds against which he has been battling so long and unsuccessfully.

This was unfortunately my condition. I had entered the medical profession with everything in my favour. My father had built up a considerable reputation for himself, and, what he prized still more, a competency as a country practitioner of the old-fashioned sort in the west of England. I was his only child, and, as he was in the habit of saying, he looked to me to carry the family name up to those dizzy heights at which he had often gazed, but upon which he had never quite been able to set his foot. A surgeon I was to be, willy-nilly, and it may have been a throw-back to the parental instinct alluded to above, that led me at once to picture myself flying at express speed across Europe in obedience to the summons of some potentate whose life and throne depended upon my dexterity and knowledge.

In due course I entered a hospital, and followed the curriculum in the orthodox fashion. It was not, however, until I was approaching the end of my student days that I was burnt with that fire of enthusiasm which was destined in future days to come perilously near consuming me altogether. Among the students of my year was a man by whose side I had often worked—with whom I had occasionally exchanged a few words, but whose intimate I could not in any way have been said to be. In appearance he was a narrow-shouldered, cadaverous, lantern-jawed fellow, with dark, restless eyes, who boasted the name of Kelleran, and was popularly supposed to be an Irishman. As I discovered later, however, he was not an Irishman at all, but hailed from the Black Country—Wolverhampton, if I remember rightly, having the right to claim the honour of his birth. His father had been the senior partner in an exceedingly wealthy firm of hardware manufacturers, and while we

1

had been in the habit of pitying and, in some instances I am afraid, of looking down upon the son on account of his supposed poverty, he was, in all probability, in a position to buy up every other man in the hospital twice over.

The average medical student is a being with whom the *world in general* has by this time been made fairly familiar. His frolics and capacity—or incapacity, as you may choose to term it—for work have been the subject of innumerable jests. If this be a true picture, then Kelleran was certainly different to the usual run of us. In his case the order was reversed: with him, work was play, and play was work; a jest was a thing unknown, and a practical joke a thing for which he allowed it to be seen that he had not the slightest tolerance.

I have already said that my father had amassed a competency. I must now add that up to a certain point he was a generous man, and for this reason my allowance, under different circumstances, would have been ample for my requirements. As ill luck would have it, however, I had got into the wrong set, and before I had been two years in the hospital was over head and ears in such a quagmire of debt and difficulties that it looked as if nothing but an absolute miracle could serve to extricate me. To my father I dared not apply: easy-going as he was on most matters, I had good reason to know that on the subject of debt he was inexorable. And yet to remain in my present condition was impossible. On every side tradesmen threatened me; my landlady's account had not been paid for weeks; while among the men of the hospital not one, but several, held my paper for sums lost at cards, the mere remembrance of which was sufficient to send a cold shiver coursing down my back every time I thought of them. From all this it will be surmised that my position was not only one of considerable difficulty but that it was also one of no little danger. Unless I could find a sum either to free myself, or at least to stave off my creditors, my career, as far as the world of medicine was concerned, might be considered at an end. Even now I can recall the horror of that period as vividly as if it were but yesterday.

Dr. Nikola's Experiment

It was on a Thursday, I remember, that the thunder-clap came. On returning to my rooms in the evening I discovered a letter awaiting me. With trembling fingers I tore open the envelope and drew out the contents. As I feared, it proved to be a demand from my most implacable creditor, a money-lender to whom I had been introduced by a fellow-student. The sum I had borrowed from him, with the assistance of a friend, was only a trifling one, but helped out by fines and other impositions it had increased to an amount which I was aware it was hopelessly impossible for me to pay. What was I to do? What could I do? Unless I settled the claim (to hope for mercy from the man himself was, to say the least of it, absurd), my friend, who, I happened to know, was himself none too well off at the moment, would be called upon to make it good. After that how should I be able to face him or any one else again? I had not a single acquaintance in the world from whom I could borrow a sum that would be half sufficient to meet it, while I dared not go down to the country and tell my father of my folly and disgrace. In vain I ransacked my brains for a loophole of escape. Then the whistle of a steamer on the river attracted my attention, filling my brain with such thoughts as it had never entertained before, and I pray, by God's mercy, may never know again. Here was a way out of my difficulty, if only I had the pluck to try it. Strangely enough, the effect it had upon me was to brace me like a draught of rare wine. This was succeeded by a coldness so intense that both mind and body were rendered callous by it. How long it lasted I cannot say; it may have been only a few seconds—it may have been an hour before consciousness returned and I found myself still standing beside the table, holding the fatal letter in my hand. Like a drunken man I fumbled my way from the room into the hot night outside. What I was going to do I had no notion. I wanted to be alone, in some place away from the crowded pavements, if possible, where I could have time to think and to determine upon my course of action.

With a tempest of rage, against I knew not what or whom, in my heart, I hurried along, up one street and down another, until I found myself panting, but unappeased, upon the Embankment opposite the Temple Gardens. All round me was the bustle and life of the great city: cabs, containing men and women in evening dress, dashed along; girls and their lovers, talking in hushed voices, went by me arm in arm; even the loafers, leaning against the stone parapet, seemed happy in comparison with my wretched self. I looked down at the dark water gliding so pleasantly along below me, and remembered that all I had to do, as soon as I was alone, was to drop over the side, and be done with my difficulties for ever. Then in a flash the real meaning of what I proposed to do occurred to me.

"You coward," I hissed, with as much vehemence and horror as if I had been addressing a real enemy instead of myself, "to think of taking this way out of your difficulty! If you kill yourself, what will become of the other man? Go to him at once and tell him everything. He has the right to know."

The argument was irresistible, and I accordingly turned upon my heel and was about to start off in quest of the individual I wanted, when I found myself confronted with no less a person than Kelleran. He was walking quickly, and swung his cane as he did so. On seeing me he stopped.

"Douglas Ingleby!" he said: "well, this is fortunate! You are just the man I wanted."

I murmured something in reply, I forget what, and was about to pass on. I had bargained without my host, however. He had been watching me with his keen dark eyes, and when he made as if he would walk with me I was not altogether surprised.

"You do not object to my accompanying you I hope?" he inquired, by way of introducing what he had to say. "I've been wanting to have a talk with you for some days past."

"I'm afraid I'm in rather a hurry just now," I answered, quickening my pace a little as I did so.

"That makes no difference at all to me," he returned. "As I think you are aware, I am a fast walker. Since you are in a hurry, let us step out."

" 'You are just the man I want to see.' "

We did so, and for something like fifty yards proceeded at a brisk pace in perfect silence. His companionship was more than I could stand, and at last I stopped and faced him.

"What is it you want with me?" I asked angrily. "Cannot you see that I am not well to-night, and would rather be alone?"

"I can see you are not quite yourself," he answered quietly, still watching me with his grave eyes. "That is exactly why I want to walk with you. A little cheerful conversation will do you good. You don't know how clever I am at adapting my manner to other people's requirements. That is the secret of our profession, my dear Ingleby, as you will some day find out."

"I shall never find it out," I replied bitterly. "I have done with medicine. I shall clear out of England, I think—go abroad, try Australia or Canada—anywhere, I don't care where, to get out of this!"

"The very thing!" he returned cheerily, but without a trace of surprise. "You couldn't do better, I'm sure. You are strong, active, full of life and ambition; just the sort of fellow to make a good colonist. It must be a grand life, that hewing and hacking a place for oneself in a new country, watching and fostering the growth of a people that may some day take its place among the powers of the earth. Ah! I like the idea. It is grand! It makes one tingle to think of it."

He threw out his arms and squared his shoulders as if he were preparing for the struggle he had so graphically described. After that we did not walk quite so fast. The man had suddenly developed a strange fascination for me, and, as he talked, I hung upon his words with a feverish interest I can scarcely account for now. By the time we reached my lodgings, I had put my trouble aside for the time being, but when I entered my sitting-room and found the envelope which had contained the fatal letter still lying upon the table, it all rushed back upon me, and with such force that I was well-nigh overwhelmed. Kelleran meanwhile had taken up his position on the hearthrug, whence he watched me with the same expression of contemplative interest upon his face to which I have before alluded.

"Hullo!" he said at last, after he had been some minutes in the house, and had had time to overhaul my meagre library, "what are these? Where did you pick them up?"

He had taken a book from the shelf, and was holding it tenderly in his hand. I recognised it as one of several volumes of a sixteenth-century work on Surgery that I had chanced upon on a bookstall in Holywell Street some months before. Its age and date had interested me, and I had bought it more out of curiosity than for any other reason. Kelleran, however, could scarcely withdraw his eyes from it.

"It's the very thing I've been wanting to make my set complete," he cried, when I had described my discovery of it. "Perhaps you don't know it, but I'm a perfect lunatic on the subject of old books. My own rooms, where, by the by, you have never been, are crammed from floor to ceiling, and still I go on buying. Let me see what else you have."

So saying, he continued his survey of the shelves, humming softly to himself as he did so, and pulling out such books as interested him, and heaping them upon the floor.

"You've the beginning of a by no means bad collection," he was kind enough to say, when he had finished. "Judging from what I see here, you must read a good deal more than most of our men."

"I'm afraid not," I answered. "The majority of these books were sent up to me from the country by my father, who thought they might be of service to me. A mistaken notion, for they take up a lot of room, and I've often wished them at Hanover."

"You have, have you? What a Goth you are!" he continued. "Well, then, I'll tell you what I'll do. If you want to get rid of them, I'll buy the lot, these old beauties included. They are really worth more than I can afford, but if you care about it, I'll make you a sporting offer of a hundred and fifty pounds for such as I've put upon the floor. What do you say?"

I could scarcely believe I heard aright. His offer was so preposterous, that I could have laughed in his face.

"My dear fellow," I cried, thinking for a moment that he must be joking with me, and feeling inclined to resent it, "what nonsense you talk! A hundred and fifty for the lot: why, they're not worth a ten-pound note, all told. The old fellows are certainly curious, but it is only fair that I should tell you that I gave five and sixpence for the set of seven volumes, complete."

"Then you got a bargain such as you'll never find again," he answered quietly. "I wish I could make as good an one every day. However, there's my offer. Take it or leave it as you please. I will give you one hundred and fifty pounds for those books, and take my chance of their value. If you are prepared to accept, I'll get a cab and take them away to-night. I've got my chequebook in my pocket, and can settle up for them on the spot."

"But, my dear Kelleran, how can you afford to give such—" Here I stopped abruptly. "I beg your pardon—I know I had no right to say such a thing."

"Don't mention it," he answered quietly. "I am not in the least offended, I assure you. I have always felt certain you fellows supposed me to be poor. As a matter of fact, however, I have the good fortune, or the ill, as I sometimes think, since it prevents my working as I should otherwise be forced to do, to be able to indulge myself to the top of my bent without fear of the consequences. But that has nothing to do with the subject at present under discussion. Will you take my price, and let me have the books, or not? I assure you I am all anxiety to get my nose inside one of those old covers before I sleep to-night."

Heaven knows I was eager enough to accept, and if you think for one moment you will see what his offer meant to me. With such a sum I could not only pay off the money-lender, but well-nigh put myself straight with the rest of my creditors. Yet all the time I had the uneasy feeling that the books were by no means worth the amount he had declared to be their value, and that he was only making me the offer out of kindness.

"If you are sure you mean it, I will accept," I said. "I am awfully hard up, and the money will be a godsend to me."

"I am rejoiced to hear it," he replied, "for in that case we shall be doing each other a mutual good turn. Now let's get them tied up. If you wouldn't mind seeing to that part of the business, I'll write the cheque and call the cab."

Ten minutes later he and his new possessions had taken their departure, and I was back once more in my room standing beside the table, just as I had done a few hours before, but with what a difference! Then I had seen no light ahead, nothing but complete darkness and dishonour; now I was a new man, and in a position to meet the majority of calls upon me. The change from the one condition to the other was more than I could bear, and when I remembered that less than sixty minutes before I was standing on that antechamber of death, the Embankment, contemplating suicide, I broke down completely, and sinking into a chair buried my face in my hands and cried like a child.

Next morning, as soon as the bank doors were open, I entered and cashed the cheque Kelleran had given me. Then, calling a cab, I made my way with a light heart, as you may suppose, to the office of the money-lender in question. His surprise at seeing me, and on learning the nature of my errand, may be better imagined than described. Having transacted my business with him, I was preparing to make my way back to the hospital, when an idea entered my head upon which I immediately acted. In something under ten minutes I stood in the bookseller's shop in Holy-well Street where I had purchased the volumes Kelleran had appeared to prize so much.

"Some weeks ago," I said to the man who came forward to serve me, "I purchased from you an old work on medicine entitled 'The Perfect Chi-surgeon, or The Art of Healing as practised in divers Ancient Countries.'"

"Seven volumes very much soiled—five and sixpence," returned the man immediately. "I remember the books."

"I'm glad of that," I answered. "Now, I want you to tell me what you would consider the real value of the work."

"If it were wanted to make up a collection it might possibly be worth a sovereign," the man replied promptly. "Otherwise, not more than we asked you for it."

"Then you don't think any one would be likely to offer a hundred pounds for it?" I inquired.

The man laughed outright.

"Not a man in the possession of his wits," he answered. "No, sir, I think I have stated the price very fairly, though of course it might fetch a few shillings more or less, according to circumstances."

"I am very much obliged to you," I said; "I simply wanted to know as a matter of curiosity."

With that I left the shop and made my way to the hospital, where I found Kelleran hard at work. He looked up at me as I entered, and nodded, but it was lunch time before I got an opportunity of speaking to him.

"Kelleran," I said, as we passed oat through the great gates, "you deceived me about those books last night. They were not worth anything like the value you put upon them."

He looked me full and fair in the face, and I saw a faint smile flicker round the corners of his mouth.

"My dear Ingleby," he said, "what a funny fellow you are, to be sure! Surely if I choose to give you what I consider the worth of the books I am at perfect liberty to do so. If you are willing to accept it, no more need be said upon the subject. The value of a thing to a man is exactly what he cares to give for it, so I have always been led to believe."

"But I am convinced you did not give it because you wanted the books. You knew I was in straits and you took that form of helping me. It was generous of you indeed, Kelleran, and I'll never forget it as long as I live. You saved me from—but there, I cannot tell you. I dare not think of it myself. There is one thing I must ask of you. I want you to keep the books and to let the amount you gave me for them be a loan, which I will repay as soon as I possibly can."

I was aware that he was a passionate man: for I had once or twice seen him fly into a rage, but never into a greater one than now.

"Let it be what you please," he cried, turning from me. "Only for pity's sake drop the subject: I've had enough of it."

With this explosion he stalked away, leaving me standing looking after him, divided between gratitude and amazement.

I have narrated this incident for two reasons: firstly because it will furnish you with a notion of my own character, which I am prepared to admit exhibits but few good points; and in the second because it will serve to introduce to you a queer individual, now a very great person, whom I shall always regard as the Good Angel of my life, and, indirectly it is true, the bringer about of the one and only real happiness I have ever known.

From the time of the episode I have just described at such length to the present day, I can safely say I have never touched a card nor owed a man a penny-piece that I was not fully prepared to pay at a moment's notice. And with this assertion I must revert to the statement made at the commencement of this chapter—the saddest a man can make. As I said then, there could be no doubt about it that I was a failure. For though I had improved in the particulars just stated, Fate was plainly against me. I worked hard and passed my examinations with comparative ease; yet it seemed to do me no good with those above me. The sacred fire of enthusiasm, which had at first been so conspicuously absent, had now taken complete hold of me; I studied night and day, grudging myself no labour, yet by some mischance everything I touched recoiled upon me, and, like the serpent of the fable, stung the hand that fostered it. Certainly I was not popular, and, since it was due almost directly to Kelleran's influence that I took to my work with such assiduity, it seems strange that I should also have to attribute my non-success to his agency. As a matter of fact, he was not a good leader to follow. From the very first he had shown himself to be a man of strange ideas. He was no follower or stickler for the orthodox; to sum him up in plainer words, he was what might be described as an experimentalist. In return, the authorities of the hospital looked somewhat askance upon him. Finally he passed out into the world, and the same term saw me appointed to the position of House Surgeon. Almost simultaneously my father died; and, to the horror of the family, an examination of his affairs proved that instead of being the wealthy man we had supposed him there was barely sufficient, when his liabilities were paid, to meet the expenses of his funeral. The shock of his death and the knowledge of the poverty to which she had been so suddenly reduced proved too much for my mother, and she followed him a few weeks later. Thus I was left, so far as I knew, without kith or kin in the world, with but few friends, no money, and the poorest possible prospects of ever making any.

To the circumstances under which I lost the position of House Surgeon I will not allude. Let it suffice that I *did* lose it, and that, although the authorities seemed to think otherwise, I am in a position to prove, whenever I desire to do so, that I was not the real culprit The effect, however, was the same. I was disgraced beyond hope of redemption, and the proud career I had mapped out for myself was now beyond my reach for good and all.

Over the next twelve months it would perhaps be better that I should draw a veil. Even now I scarcely like to think of them. It is enough for me to say that for upwards of a month I remained in London, searching high and low for employment. This, however, was easier looked for than discovered. Try how I would, I could hear of nothing. Then, wearying of the struggle, I accepted an offer made me, and left England as surgeon on board an outward-bound passenger steamer for Australia.

Ill luck, however, still pursued me, for at the end of my second voyage the Company went into liquidation, and its vessels were sold. I shipped on board another boat in a similar capacity, made two voyages in her to the Cape, where on a friend's advice I bade her goodbye, and started for Ashanti as surgeon to an Inland Trading Company. While there I was wounded in the neck by a spear, was compelled to leave the Company's service, and eventually found myself back once more in London tramping the streets in search of employment. Fortunately, however, I had managed to save a small sum from my pay, so that I was not altogether destitute; but it was not long before this was exhausted, and then things looked blacker than they had ever done before. What to do I knew not. I had long since cast *my* pride to the winds, and was now prepared to take anything, no matter what. Then an idea struck me, and on it I acted.

Leaving my lodgings on the Surrey side of the river, I crossed Blackfriars Bridge, and made my way along the Embankment in a westerly direction. As I went I could not help contrasting my present appearance with that I had shown on the last occasion I had walked that way. Then I had been as spruce and neat as a man could well be; boasted a good coat to my back and a new hat upon my head. Now, however, the coat and hat, instead of speaking for my prosperity, as at one time they might have done, bore unmistakable evidence of the disastrous change which had taken place in my fortunes. Indeed, if the truth must be confessed, I was about as sorry a specimen of the professional man as could be found in the length and breadth of the Metropolis.

2

" I was about as sorry a specimen of the professional man as could be found."

Reaching the thoroughfare in which I had heard that Kelleran had taken up his abode, I cast about me for a means of ascertaining his number. Compared with that in which I myself resided, this was a street of palaces, but it seemed to me I could read the characters of the various tenants in the appearance of each house-front. The particular one before which I was standing at the moment was frivolous in the extreme: the front door was artistically painted, an elaborate knocker ornamented the centre panel, while the windows were without exception curtained with dainty expensive stuffs. Everything pointed to the mistress being a lady of fashion; and having put one thing and another together, I felt convinced I should not find my friend there. The next I came to was a residence of more substantial type. Here everything was solid and plain, even to the borders of severity. If I could sum up the owner, he was a successful man, a lawyer for choice, a bachelor, and possibly, and even probably, a bigot on matters of religion. He would have two or three friends—not more—all of whom would be advanced in years, and, like himself, successful men of business. He would be able to appreciate a glass of dry sherry, and would have nothing to do with anything that did not bear the impress of a gilt-edged security. As neither of these houses seemed to suggest that they would be likely to know anything of the man I wanted, I made my way further down the street, looking about me as I proceeded. At last I came to a standstill before one that I was prepared to swear was inhabited by my old friend. His character was stamped unmistakably upon every inch of it: the untidy windows, the pile of books upon a table in the bow, the marks upon the front door where his impatient foot had often pressed while he turned his latchkey: all these spoke of Kelleran, and I was certain my instinct was not misleading me. Ascending the steps, I rang the bell. It was answered by a tall and somewhat austere woman of between forty and fifty years of age, upon whom a coquettish frilled apron and cap sat with incongruous effect. As I afterwards learnt, she had been Kelleran's nurse in bygone years, and since he had become a householder had taken charge of his domestic arrangements, and ruled both himself and his maidservants with a rod of iron.

"Would you be kind enough to inform me if Mr. Kelleran is at home?" I asked, after we had taken stock of each other.

"He has been abroad for more than three months," the woman answered abruptly. Then, seeing the disappointment upon my face, she added, "I don't know when we may expect him home. He may be here on Saturday, and it's just possible we may not see him for two or three weeks to come. But perhaps you'll not mind telling me what your business with him may be?"

"It is not very important," I answered humbly, feeling that my position was, to say the least of it, an invidious one. "I am an old friend, and I wanted to see him for a few minutes. Since, however, he is not at home, it does not matter, I assure you. I shall have other opportunities of communicating with him. At the same time, you might be kind enough to tell him I called."

"You'd better let me know your name first," she replied, with a look that suggested as plainly as any words could speak that she did not for an instant believe my assertion that I was a friend of her master's.

"My name is Ingleby," I said. "Mr. Kelleran will be sure to remember me. We were at the same hospital."

She gave a scornful sniff as if such a thing would be very unlikely, and then made as if she would shut the door in my face. I was not, however, to be put off in this fashion. Taking a card from my pocket, one of the last I possessed, I scrawled my name and present address upon it and handed it to her.

"Perhaps if you will show that to Mr. Kelleran he would not mind writing to me when he comes home," I said. "That is where I am living just now."

She glanced at the card, and, noting the locality, sniffed even more scornfully than before. It was evident that this was the only thing wanting to confirm the bad impression I had already created in her mind. For some seconds there was an ominous silence.

"Like a ministering angel she half led, half supported
me into the house."

"Very well," she answered, at length, "I'll give it to him. But—why, Heaven save us! what's the matter? You're as white as a sheet. Why didn't you say you were feeling ill?"

I had been running it rather close for more than a week past, and the news that Kelleran, my last hope, was absent from England had unnerved me altogether. A sudden giddiness seized me, and I believe I should have fallen to the ground had I not clutched at the railings by my side. It was then that the real nature of the woman became apparent. Like a ministering angel she half led, half supported me into the house, and seated me on a chair in the somewhat sparsely furnished hall.

"Friend of the master, or no friend," I heard her say to herself, "I'll take the risk of it."

I heard no more, for my senses had left me. When they returned I found myself lying upon a sofa in Kelleran's study, the housekeeper standing by my side, and a maidservant casting sympathetic glances at me from the doorway.

"I'm afraid I have put you to a lot of trouble," I said, as soon as I had recovered myself sufficiently to speak. "I cannot think what made me go off like that. I have never done such a thing in my life before."

"You can't think?" queried the woman, with a curious intonation that was not lost upon me. "Then it's very plain you've not much wit about you. I think, young man, I could make a very good guess at the truth if I wanted to. How-somever, let that be as it may, I'll put a bit of it right before you leave this house, or my name's not what it is." Then turning to the maid, who was still watching me, she continued sharply, "Be off about your business, miss, and do as I told you. Are you going to waste all the afternoon standing there staring about you like a baby?"

The girl tossed her head and disappeared, only to return a few minutes later with a tray, upon which was set out a substantial meal of cold meat.

On the old woman's ordering me to do so I sat down to it, and dined as I had not done for months past.

"There," she said, with an air of triumph as I finished, "that will make a new man of you." Then, having done all she could for me, and repenting, perhaps, of the leniency she had shown me, she returned to her former abrupt demeanour, and informed me, in terms there was no mistaking, that her time was valuable, and it behoved me to be off about my business as soon as possible. While she had been speaking, my eyes had travelled round the room until they lighted upon the mantelpiece (it was covered with pipes, books, photographs, and all the innumerable odds and ends that accumulate in a bachelor's apartment), where I discovered my own portrait with several others. I remembered having given it to Kelleran two years before. It was not a very good one, but with its assistance I proposed to establish my identity and prove to my stern benefactress that I was not altogether the impostor she believed me to be.

"I cannot tell you how grateful I am to you for all you have done," I said, as I rose and prepared to take my departure from the house. "At the same time I am very much afraid you do not altogether believe that I am the friend of your master's that I pretend to be."

"Tut, tut!" she answered. "If I were in your place I'd say no more about that. Least said soonest mended, is my motto. I trust, however, I'm a Christian woman, and do my best to help folk in distress. But I've warned ye already that I've eyes in my head and wit enough to tell what's o'clock just as well as my neighbours. Why, bless my soul, you don't think I've been all my years in the world without knowing what's what, or who's who?"

She paused as if for breath; and, embracing the opportunity, I crossed the room and took from the chimneypiece the photograph to which I have just alluded.

"Possibly this may help to reassure you," I said, as I placed it before her. "I do not think I have changed so much, since it was taken, that you should fail to recognise me."

"It's Ingleby this and Ingleby that from morning till night."

She picked up the photo and looked at it, reading the signature at the bottom with a puzzled face.

"Heaven save us, so it *is*!" she cried, when the meaning of it dawned upon her. "You are Mr. Ingleby, after all? Well, I am a softy, to be sure. I thought you were trying to take me in. So many people come here asking to see him, saying they were at the hospital with him that you've got to be more than careful. If I'd have thought it really was you, I'd have bitten my tongue out before I'd have said what I did. Why, sir, the master talks of you to this day: it's Ingleby this, and Ingleby that, from morning till night. Many's the time he's made inquiries from gentlemen who've been here, in the hopes of finding out what has become of ye."

"God bless him!" I said, my heart warming at the news that he had not forgotten me. "We were the best of friends once."

"But, Mr. Ingleby," continued the old woman after a pause, "if you'll allow me to say so, I don't like to see you like this. You must have seen *a* lot of trouble, sir, to have got in such a state."

"The world has not treated me very kindly," I answered, with an attempt at a smile, "but I'll tell Kelleran all about it when I see him. You think it is possible he may be home on Saturday?"

"I hope so, sir, I'm sure," she replied. "You may be certain I'll give him your address, and tell him you've called, the moment I see him."

I thanked her again for her trouble, and took my departure, feeling a very different man as I went down the steps and turned my face citywards. In my own heart I felt certain Kelleran would do something to help me. Had I known, however, what that something was destined to be, I wonder whether I should have awaited his coming with such eagerness.

As it transpired, it was on the Friday following my call at his house that, on returning to my lodgings after another day's fruitless search for employment, I found the following letter awaiting me. The handwriting was as familiar to me as my own, and it may be imagined with what eagerness I tore open the envelope and scanned the contents. It ran:

"MY DEAR INGLEBY,

"It was a pleasant welcome home to find that you are in England once more. I am sorry, however, to learn from my housekeeper that affairs have not been prospering with you. This must be remedied, and at once. I flatter myself I am just the man to do it. It is possible you may consider me unfeeling when I say that there never was such luck as your being in want of employment at this particular moment. I've a billet standing ready and waiting for you; one of the very sort you are fitted for, and one that you will enjoy, unless you have lost your former tastes and inclinations. You have never met Dr. Nikola, but you must do so without delay. I tell you, Ingleby, he is the most wonderful man with whom I have ever been brought in contact. We chanced upon each other in St. Petersburg three months ago, and since then he's fascinated me as no other man has ever done. I have spoken of you to him, and in consequence he dines with me to-night in the hope of meeting you. Whatever else you do, therefore, do not fail to put in an appearance. You cannot guess the magnitude of the experiment upon which he is at work. At first glance, and in any other man, it would seem incredible, impossible, I might almost say absurd. When, however, you have seen him, I venture to think you will not doubt that he will carry it through. Let me count upon you to-night, then, at seven.

"Always your friend,

"Andrew Fairfax Kelleran."

I read the letter again. What did it mean? At any rate, it contained a ray of hope. It would have to be a very curious billet, I told myself, under present circumstances, that I would refuse. But who was this extraordinary individual, Dr Nikola, who seemed to have exercised such a fascination over my enthusiastic friend? Well, that I had to find out for myself.

CHAPTER II. A NEW IMPETUS

THE clocks in the neighbourhood had scarcely ceased striking as I ascended the steps of Kelleran's house and rang the bell. Even had he not been so impressive in his invitation there was small likelihood of my forgetting the appointment I had been waiting for it, hour by hour, with an impatience that can only be understood when I say that each one was bringing me nearer the only satisfying meal I had had since I last visited his abode.

The door was opened to me by the same faithful housekeeper who had proved herself such a ministering angel on the previous occasion. She greeted me as an old friend, but with a greater respect than she had shown when we had last talked together. This did not prevent her, however, from casting a scrutinising eye over me, as much as to say, "You look a bit more respectable, my lad, but your coat is very faded at the seams, your collar is frayed at the edge, and you sniff the smell of dinner as if you have not had a decent meal for longer than you care to think about"; all of which, had she put it into so many words, would have been perfectly true.

"Step inside," she said; "Mr. Kelleran's waiting for you in the study, I know." Then sinking her voice to a whisper she added: "There's duck and green peas for dinner, and as soon as the other gentleman arrives I shall tell cook to dish. He'll not be long now."

What answer I should have returned I cannot say, but as she finished speaking a door farther down the passage opened, and my old friend made his appearance, with the same impetuosity that always characterised him.

"Ingleby, my dear fellow," he cried, as he ran with outstretched hand to greet me, "I cannot tell you how pleased I am to see you again. It seems years since I last set eyes on you. Come in here; I want to have a good look at you. We've hundreds of things to say to each other, and heaps of questions to ask, haven't we? And, by Jove, we must look sharp about it too, for in a few minutes Nikola will be here. I asked him to come at a quarter past seven, in order that we might have a little time alone together first."

So saying, he led me into his study, the same in which I had returned to my senses after my fainting fit a few days before, and when he had done so he bade me seat myself in an easy chair.

"You can't think how good it is to see you again, Kelleran," I said, as soon as I could get in a word. "I had begun to think myself forgotten by all my friends."

"Bosh!" was his uncompromising reply. "Talk about your friends— why, you never know who they are till you're in trouble! At least, that's what I think. And, by the way, let me tell you that you *do* look a bit pulled down. I wonder what idiocy you've been up to since I saw you last. Tell me about it. You won't smoke a cigarette before dinner? Very good! now fire away!"

Thus encouraged, I told him in a few words all that had befallen me since we had last met. While I was talking he stood before me, his face lit up with interest, and to all intents and purposes as absorbed in my story as if it had been his own.

"Well, well, thank goodness it is all over now," he said, when I had brought my tale to a conclusion. "I think I've found you a billet that will suit you admirably, and if you play your cards well there's no saying to what it may not lead. Nikola is the most marvellous man in the world, as you will admit when you have seen him. I, for one, have never met anybody like him; and as for this new scheme of his, why, if he brings it off, I give you my word it will revolutionise Science."

I was too well acquainted with my friend's enthusiastic way of talking to be surprised at it; at the same time I was thoroughly conversant with his cleverness, and for this reason I was prepared to believe that, if he thought well of any scheme, there must be something out of the common in it.

"But what is this wonderful idea?" I asked, scarcely able to contain my longing, as the fumes of dinner penetrated to us from the regions below. "And how am I affected by it?"

"That I must leave for Dr. Nikola to tell you himself," Kelleran replied. "Let it suffice for the moment that I envy you your opportunity. I believe if I had been able to avail myself of the chance he offered me of going into it with him, I should have been compelled to sacrifice you. But there, you will hear all about it in good time, for if I am not mistaken that is his cab drawing up outside now. It is one of his peculiarities to be always punctual to the moment What do you make the right time by your watch?"

I was obliged to confess that I possessed no watch. It had been turned into the necessaries of existence long since. Kelleran must have realised what was passing in my mind, though he pretended not to have noticed it; at any rate he said, "I make it a quarter past seven to the minute, and I am prepared to wager that's our man."

A bell rang, and almost before the sound of it had died away the study door opened, and the housekeeper, with a look of awe upon her face which had not been there when she addressed me, announced "Dr. Nikola."

Looking back on it now, I find that, in spite of all that has happened since, my impressions of that moment are as fresh and clear as if it were but yesterday. I can see the tall, lithe figure of this extraordinary man, his sallow face, and his piercing black eyes steadfastly regarding me, as if he were trying to determine whether or not I was capable of assisting him in the work upon which he was so exhaustively engaged. Never before had I seen such eyes; they seemed to look me through and through, and to read my inmost thoughts.

"This gentleman, my dear Kelleran," he began, after they had shaken hands, and without waiting for me to be introduced to him, "should be your friend Ingleby, of whom you have so often spoken to me. How do you do, Mr. Ingleby? I don't think there is much doubt but that we shall work admirably together. You have lately been in Ashanti, I perceive."

I admitted that I had, and went on to inquire how he had become aware of it; for as Kelleran had not known it until a few minutes before, I did not see how he could be acquainted with the fact.

"It is not a very difficult thing to tell," he answered, with a smile at my astonishment, "seeing that you carry about with you the mark of a Gwato spear. If it were necessary I could tell you some more things that would surprise you: for instance, I could tell you that the man who cut the said spear out for you was an amateur at his work, that he was left-handed, that he was short-sighted, and that he was recovering from malaria at the time. All this is plain to the eye; but I see our friend Kelleran fancies his dinner is getting cold, so we had better postpone our investigations for a more convenient opportunity."

We accordingly left the study and proceeded to the dining-room. All day long I had been looking forward to that moment with the eagerness of a starving man, yet when it arrived I scarcely touched anything. If the truth must be confessed, there was something about this man that made me forget such mundane matters as mere eating and drinking. And I noticed that Nikola himself was even more abstemious. For this reason, save for the fact that he himself enjoyed it, the bountiful spread Kelleran had arranged for us was completely wasted.

During the progress of the meal no mention was made of the great experiment upon which our host had informed me Nikola was engaged. Our conversation was mainly devoted to travel. Nikola, I soon discovered, had been everywhere, and had seen everything. There appeared to be no place on the face of the habitable globe with which he was not acquainted, and of which he could not speak with the authority of an old resident. China, India, Australia, South America, North, South, East, and West Africa, were as familiar to him as Piccadilly, and it was in connection with one of the last-named Continents that a curious incident occurred.

We had been discussing various cases of catalepsy; and to illustrate an argument he was adducing, Kelleran narrated a curious instance of lethargy with which he had become acquainted in Southern Russia. While he was speaking I noticed that Nikola's face wore an expression that was partly one of derision and partly of amusement.

"I think I can furnish you with an instance that is even more extraordinary," I said, when our host had finished; and as I did so, Nikola leaned a little towards me. "In fairness to your argument, however, Kelleran, I must admit that while it comes under the same category, the malady in question confines itself almost exclusively to the black races on the West Coast of Africa."

"You refer to the Sleeping Sickness, I presume?" said Nikola, whose eyes were fixed upon me, and who was paying the greatest attention to all I said.

"Exactly—the Sleeping Sickness," I answered. "I was fortunate enough to see several instances of it when I was on the West Coast, though the one to which I am referring did not come before me personally, but was described to me by a man, a rather curious character, who happened to be in the district at the time. The negro in question, a fine healthy fellow of about twenty years of age, was servant to a Portuguese trader at Cape Coast Castle. He had been up country on some trading expedition or other, and during the whole time had enjoyed the very best of health. For the first few days after his return to the coast, however, he was unusually depressed. Slight swelling of the cervical glands set in, accompanied by a tendency to fall asleep at any time. This somnolency gradually increased; cutaneous stimulation was tried, at first with comparative success; the symptoms, however, soon recurred, the periods of sleep became longer and more frequent, until at last the patient could scarcely have been said to be ever awake. The case, so my informant said, was an extremely interesting one."

"But what was the result?" inquired Kelleran, a little impatiently. "You have not told us to what all this is leading."

"Well, the result was that in due course the patient became extremely emaciated—a perfect skeleton, in fact. He would take no food, answered no questions, and did not open his eyes from morning till night. To make a long story short, just as my informant was beginning to think that the end was approaching, there appeared in Cape Coast Castle a mysterious stranger who put forward claims to a knowledge of medicine. He forgathered with my man, and after a while obtained permission to try his hand upon the negro."

"And killed him at once, of course?"

"Nothing of the sort. The result was one that you will scarcely credit. The whole business was most irregular, I believe, but my friend was not likely to worry himself much about that. This new man had his own pharmacopoeia—a collection of essences in small bottles, more like what they used in the Middle Ages than anything else, I should imagine. Having obtained possession of the patient, he carried him away to a hut outside the town and took him in hand there and then.

"The man who told me about it, and who, I should have said, had had a good experience of the disease, assured me that he was as certain as any one possibly could be that the chap could not live out the week; and yet when the new-comer, ten days later, invited him to visit the hut, there was the man acting as his servant, waiting at table, if you please, and to all intents and purposes, though very thin, as well as ever he had been in his life."

"But, my dear fellow," protested Kelleran, "Guerin says that out of the 148 cases that came under his notice 148 died."

"I can't help what Guerin says," I answered, a little warmly I am afraid. "I am only telling you what my friend told me. He gave me his word of honour that the result was as he described. The strangest part of the whole business, however, has yet to be told. It appears that the man had not only cured the fellow, but that he had the power of returning him to the condition in which he found him, at will. It wasn't hypnotism, but what it was is more that I can say. My informant described it to me as being about the uncanniest performance he had ever witnessed."

"In what way?" asked Kelleran. "Furnish us with a more detailed account. There was a time when you were a famous hand at a diagnosis."

"I would willingly do so," I answered; "unfortunately, however, I can't remember it all. It appears that he was always saying the most mysterious things and putting the strangest questions. On one occasion he asked my friend, as they were standing by the negro's bedside, if there was any one whose image he would care to see? Merton at first thought he was making fun of him, but seeing that he was in earnest he considered for a moment, and eventually answered that he would very much like to see the portrait of an old shipmate who had perished at sea some six or seven years prior to his arrival on the West Coast. As soon as he had said this the man stooped over the bed and opened the sleeping nigger's eyes. 'Examine the retina, he said, and I think you will see what you want.' My friend looked."

"With what result?" inquired Kelleran. Nikola said nothing, but smiled, as I thought, a trifle sceptically.

"It seems an absurd thing to say, I know," I continued, "but he swore to me that he had before him the exact picture of the man he had referred to; and what is more, standing on the deck of the steamer just as he had last seen him. It was as clear and distinct as if it had been a photograph."

"And all the time the negro was asleep?"

"Fast asleep!" I answered.

"I should very much like to meet your friend," said Kelleran emphatically. "A man with an imagination like that must be an exceedingly interesting companion. But seriously, my dear Ingleby, you don't mean to say you wish us to believe that all this really happened?"

"I am telling you what he told me," I answered. "I cannot swear to the truth of it, of course, but I will go so far as to say that I do not think he was intentionally deceiving me."

Kelleran shrugged his shoulders incredulously, and for some moments an uncomfortable silence ensued. This was broken by Nikola.

"My dear Kelleran," he said, "I don't think you are altogether fair to our friend Ingleby. As he admits, he was only speaking on hearsay, and under these circumstances he might very easily have been deceived. Fortunately, however, for the sake of his reputation I am in a position to corroborate all he has said."

"The deuce you are!" cried Kelleran; while I was too much astonished to speak, and could only stare at him in complete surprise. "What on earth do you mean? Pray explain."

"I can only do so by saying that I was the man who did this apparently wonderful thing."

Kelleran and I continued to stare at him in amazement. It was too absurd. Could he be laughing at us? And yet his face was serious enough.

"You do not seem to credit my assertion," said Nikola, quietly. "And yet I assure you it is correct. I was the mysterious individual who appeared in Cape Coast Castle, who brought with him his own pharmacopoeia, and who wrought the miracle which your friend appears to have considered so wonderful."

"The coincidence is too extraordinary," I answered, as if in protest.

"Coincidences are necessarily extraordinary," Nikola replied. "I do not see that this one is more so than usual."

"And the miracle?"

"Was in reality no miracle at all," he answered; "it was merely the logical outcome of a perfectly natural process. Pray do not look so incredulous. I am aware that my statement is difficult to believe, but I assure you, my dear Ingleby, that it is quite true. However, proof is always better than mere assertion, so, since you are still sceptical, let me make my position right with you. For reasons that will be self-evident I cannot produce the effect in a negro's eye, but I can do so in a way that will strike you as being scarcely less extraordinary. If you will draw up your chairs I will endeavour to explain."

Needless to remark, we did as he desired; and when we were seated on either side of him waited for the manifestation he had promised us.

Taking a small silver box, but little larger than a card-case, from his pocket, he opened it and tipped what might have been a teaspoonful of black powder into the centre of a dessert plate. I watched it closely, in the hope of being able to discover of what it was composed. My efforts, however, were unavailing. It was black, as I have already said, and from a distance resembled powdered charcoal. This, however, it could not have been, by reason of its strange liquidity, which was as great as that of quicksilver, and which only came into operation when it had been exposed to the air for some minutes. Hither and thither the stuff ran about the dish, and I noticed that as it did so it gradually lost its original sombre hue and took to itself a variety of colours that were as brilliant as the component tints of the spectrum. These scintillated and quivered till the eyes were almost blinded by their radiance, and yet they riveted the attention in such a manner that it was well-nigh, if not quite, impossible to look away or to think of anything else. In vain I tried to calm myself, in order that I might be a cool and collected observer of what was taking place. Whether there was any perfume thrown off by the stuff upon the plate I cannot say, but as I watched it my head began to swim and my eyelids felt as heavy as lead. That this was not fancy upon my part is borne out by the fact that Kelleran afterwards confessed to me that he experienced exactly the same sensations. Nikola, however, was still manipulating the dish, turning it this way and that, as if he were anxious to produce as many varieties of colour as possible in a given time. It must have been upwards of five minutes before he spoke. As he did so he gave the plate an extra tilt, so that the mixture ran down to one side. It was now a deep purple in colour.

"I think if you will look into the centre of the fluid you will see something that will go a long way towards convincing you of the truth of the assertion I made just now," he said quietly, but without turning his head to look at me.

I looked as he desired, but at first could see nothing save the mixture itself, which was fast turning from purple to blue. This blue grew gradually paler; and as I watched, to my astonishment, a picture formed itself before my eyes. I saw a long wooden house, surrounded on all sides by a deep verandah. The latter was covered with a beautiful flowering creeper. On either side of the dwelling was a grove of palms, and to the right, showing like a pool of dazzling quicksilver between the trees, was the sea. And pervading everything was the sensation of intense heat. At first glance I could not recall the house, but it was not long before I recognised the residence of the man who had told me the story which had occasioned this looked at it again, and could even see the window of the room in which I had recovered from my first severe attack of fever, and from which I never thought to have emerged alive. With the sight of it the recollection of that miserable time came back to me, and Kelleran and even his friend Nikola were, for the moment, forgotten.

"From the expression upon your face I gather that you know the place," said Nikola, after I had been watching it for a few moments. "Now look into the verandah, and tell me if you recognise the two men you see seated there."

I looked again, and saw that one was myself, while the other, the man who was leaning against the verandah rail smoking a cigar, was the owner of the house itself. There could be no mistake about it. The whole scene was as plain before my eyes as if it had been a photograph taken on the spot.

"There," said Nikola, with a little note of triumph in his voice, "I hope that will convince you that when I say I can do a thing, I mean it"

So saying he tilted the saucer, and the picture vanished in a whirl of colour. I tried to protest, but before I had time to say anything the liquid had in some strange fashion resolved itself once more into a powder, Nikola had tipped it back into the silver box, and Kelleran and I were left to put the best explanation we could upon it. We looked at each other, and, feeling that I could not make head or tail of what I had seen, I waited for him to speak.

"I never saw such a thing in my life," he cried, when he had found sufficient voice. "If any one had told me that such a thing was possible I would not have believed him. I can scarcely credit the evidence of my senses now."

"In fact, you feel towards the little exhibition I have just given you very much as you did to Ingleby's story a quarter of an hour ago," said Nikola. "What a doubting world it is, to be sure! The same world which ridiculed the notion that there could be anything in vaccination, in the steam engine, in chloroform, the telegraph, the telephone, or the phonograph. For how many years has it scoffed at the power of hypnotism! How many of our cleverest scientists fifty years ago could have foretold the discovery of argon, or the possibility of being able to telegraph without the aid of wires? And because the little world of to-day knows these things and has survived the wonder of them, it is convinced it has attained the end of wisdom. The folly of it! To-night I have shown you something for which less than a hundred years ago I should have been stoned as a wizard. At my death the secret will be given to the world, and the world, when it has recovered from its astonishment, will say, 'How very simple! why did no one discover it before?' I tell you, gentlemen," Nikola continued, rising and standing before the fireplace, "that we three, to-night, are standing on the threshold of a discovery which will shake the world to its foundations."

When he had moved, Kelleran and I had also pushed back our chairs from the table, and were now watching him as if turned to stone. The sacred fire of enthusiasm, which I thought had left me for ever, was once more kindling in my breast, and I hung upon his words as if I were afraid I might lose even a breath that escaped his lips. As for Nikola himself, his usually pallid face was aglow with excitement.

"The story is as old as the hills," he began. "Ever since the days when our first parents trod the earth there have been men who have aimed at discovering a means of lengthening the span of life. From the very infancy of science, the wisest and cleverest have devoted their lives to the study of the human body, in the hope of mastering its secret. Assisting in the search for that particular something which was to revolutionise the world, we find Zosimus the Theban, the Jewess Maria, the Arabian Geber, Hermes Trismegistus, Linnaeus, Berzelius, Cuvier, Raymond Lully, Paracelsus, Roger Bacon, De Lisle, Albertus Magnus, and even Dr. Price. Each in his turn quarried in the mountain of Wisdom, and died having failed to discover the hidden treasure for which he sought. And why? Because, egotistical as it may seem on my part to say so, they did not seek in the right place. They commenced at the wrong point, and worked from it in the wrong direction. But if they failed to find what they wanted, they at least rendered good service to those who were to follow after, for from every failure something new was learned. For my part I have studied the subject in every form, in every detail. For more years than I can tell you, I have lived for it, dreamed of it, fought for it, and overcome obstacles of the very existence of which no man could dream. The work of my predecessors is known to me; I have studied their writings, and tested their experiments to the last particular. All the knowledge that modern science has accumulated I have acquired. The magic of the East I have explored and tested to the uttermost. Three years ago I visited Thibet under extraordinary circumstances. There, in a certain place, inaccessible to the ordinary man, and at the risk of my own life and that of the brave man who accompanied me, I obtained the information which was destined to prove the coping-stone of the great discovery I have since made. Only two things were wanting then to . . complete the whole and to enable me to get to work. One of these I had just found in St. Petersburg when I first met you, Kelleran; the other I discovered three weeks ago. It has been a long and tedious search, but such labour only makes success the sweeter. The machinery is now prepared; all that remains is to fit the various parts together. In six months' time, if all goes well, I will have a man walking upon this earth who, under certain conditions, shall live a thousand years."

I could scarcely believe that I heard aright. Was the man deliberately asking us to believe that he had really found the way to prolong human life indefinitely? It sounded very much like it, and yet this was the Nineteenth Century and . . . But at this point I ceased my speculations. Had I not, only that evening, witnessed an exhibition of his marvellous powers? If he had penetrated so far into the Unknowable—at least what we considered the unknowable—as to be able to work such a miracle, why should we doubt that he could carry out what he was now professing to be able to do?

"And when shall we be permitted to hear the result of your labours?" asked Kelleran with a humility that was surprising in a man usually so self-assertive.

"Who can say?" asked Nikola. "These things are more or less dependent on Time. It may be only a short period before I am ready; on the other hand a lifetime may elapse. The process is above all a gradual one, and to hurry it might be to spoil everything. And now, my dear Kelleran, with your permission I will bid you good-night. I leave for the North at daybreak, and I have much to do before I go. If I am not taking you away too soon, Ingleby, perhaps you would not mind walking a short distance with me. I have a good deal to say to you."

"I shall be very pleased," I answered; and the look that Kelleran gave me showed me that he considered my decision a wise one.

"In that case come along," said Nikola. "Good-night, Kelleran, and many thanks for the introduction you have given me. I feel quite sure Ingleby and I will get on admirably together."

He shook hands with Kelleran, and passed into the hall, leaving me alone with the man who had proved my benefactor for the second time in my life.

"Good-night, old fellow," I said, as I shook him by the hand. "I cannot thank you sufficiently for your goodness in putting me in the way of this billet. It has given me another chance, and I shan't forget your kindness as long as I live."

"Don't be absurd," Kelleran answered. "You take things too seriously. I feel sure the advantage is as much Nikola's as yours. He's a wonderful man, and you're the very fellow he requires: between you, you ought to be able to bring about something that will upset the calculations of certain pompous old fossils of our acquaintance. Good-night, and good luck to you!"

So saying, he let us out by the front door, and stood upon the doorstep watching us as we walked down the street. It was an exquisite night. The moon was almost at the full, and her mellow rays made the street almost as light as day. My companion and I walked for some distance in silence. He did not speak, and I already entertained too much respect for him to interrupt his reverie. More than once I glanced at his tall, graceful figure, and the admirably shaped head, which seemed such a fitting case for the extraordinary brain within.

"As I said just now," he began at length, as if he were continuing a conversation which had been suddenly interrupted, "I leave at daybreak for the North of England. For the purposes of the experiment I am about to make, it is vitally necessary that I should possess a residence far removed from other people, where I should not run any risk of being disturbed. For this reason I have purchased Allerdeyne Castle, in Northumberland, a fine old place overlooking the North Sea. It is by no means an easy spot to get at, and should suit my purposes admirably. I shall not see you before I go, so that whatever I have to say had better be said at once. To begin with, I presume you have made up your mind to assist me in the work I am about to undertake?"

"If you consider me competent," I answered, "I shall be only too glad to do so."

"Kelleran has assured me that I could not have a better assistant," he replied, "and I am willing to take you upon his recommendation. If you have no objection to bring forward, we may as well consider the matter settled. Have you any idea as to the remuneration you will require?"

I answered that I had not, and that I would leave it to him to give me whatever he considered fair. In reply he named a sum that almost took my breath away. I remarked that I should be satisfied with half the amount, whereupon he laughed good-humouredly.

"I'm afraid we're neither of us good business men," he said. "By all the laws of trade, on finding that I offered you more than you expected, you should have stood out for twice as much. Still, I like you all the better for your modesty. Now my road turns off here, and I will bid you good-night. In an hour I will send my servant to you with a letter containing full instructions. I need scarcely say that I am sure you will carry them out to the letter."

"I will do so, come what may," I answered seriously.

"Then good-night," he said, and held out his hand to me. "All being well, we shall meet again in two or three days."

"Good-night," I replied.

Then, with a wave of his hand to me, he sprang into a hansom which he had called up to the pavement, gave the direction to the driver, and a moment later was round the corner and out of sight. After he had gone, I continued my homeward journey.

I had not been in the house an hour before I was informed that some one was at the door desiring to see me. I accordingly hurried downstairs, to find myself face to face with the most extraordinary individual I have ever seen in my life. At first glance I scarcely knew what to make of him, but when the light from the hall lamp fell upon his face, I saw that he was a Chinaman, and the ugliest I have ever seen in all my experience of the Mongolian race. His eyes squinted terribly, and a portion of his nose was missing. It was the sort of face one sees in a nightmare, and, accustomed as I was by my profession to horrible sights, I must admit my gorge rose at him. At first it did not occur to me to connect him with Nikola.

"Do you want to see me?" I inquired, in some astonishment.

He nodded his head, but did not speak. "What is it about?" I continued. He uttered a peculiar grunt, and produced a letter and a small box from his pocket, both of which he handed to me. I understood immediately from whom he came. Signing to him to remain where he was until I could tell him whether there was an answer, I turned into the house and opened the letter. Having read it, I returned to the front door.

"You can tell Dr. Nikola that I will be sure to attend to it," I said. "You savee?"

He nodded his head, and next moment was on his way down the street. When he was out of sight I returned to my bedroom, and, lighting the gas, once more perused the communication I had received. As I did so a piece of paper fell from between the leaves. I picked it up, to discover that it was a cheque for one hundred pounds payable to myself. The letter ran:

"My dear Ingleby,

"According to the promise I made you this evening, I am sending you herewith by my Chinese servant, your instructions, as clearly worked out as I can make them. To begin with, I want you to remain in town until Monday next. On the morning of that day, if all goes well, you will be advised by the agent of the Company in London of the arrival in the river of the steamship *Dona Mercedes*, bound from Cadiz to Newcastle. On receipt of that information you will be good enough to board her and to inquire for Don Miguel de Moreno and his great-granddaughter, who are passengers by the boat to England. I have already arranged with the Company for your passage, so you need have no anxiety upon that score.

"You will find the Don a very old man, and I beg that you will take the greatest possible care of him. For this reason I have sent you the accompanying drugs, each of which is labelled with the fullest instructions. They should not be made use of unless occasion absolutely requires."

(Here followed a list of the various symptoms for which I was to watch, and an exhaustive *resume* of the treatment I was to employ in the event of certain contingencies arising.)

"On the arrival of the vessel in Newcastle"—the letter continued—"I will communicate with you again. In the meantime I send you what I think will serve to pay your expenses until we meet.

"Believe me,

"Your sincere friend,

"Nikola."

"P.S.—One last word of warning. Should you by any chance be brought into contact with a certain Mongolian of very sinister appearance, with half an ear missing, have nothing whatsoever to do with him. Keep out of his way, and above all let him know nothing of your connection with myself. This, I beg you to believe, is no idle warning, for all our lives depend upon it."

Having thoroughly mastered the contents of this curious epistle, I turned my attention to the parcel which accompanied it. This I discovered was made up of a number of small packets evidently containing powders, and two-ounce phials of some tasteless and scentless liquid, to which I was quite unable to assign a name.

Once more I glanced at the letter, in order to make sure of the name of the man whose guardian I was destined for the future to be. De Moreno was the name, and it was his granddaughter who was accompanying him. In an idle, dreamy way, I wondered what the latter would prove to be like. For some reason or another I found myself thinking a good deal of her, and when I fell asleep that night it was to dream that she was standing before me with outstretched hands, imploring me to save her not only from a certain one-eared Chinaman, but also from Nikola himself.

CHAPTER III. THE MYSTERIOUS CHINAMAN

AFTER my meeting with Nikola at Kelleran's house, it was a new prospect that life opened up for me. I confronted the future with a smiling face, and no longer told myself, as I had done so often of late, that Failure and I were inseparable companions, and for any success I might hope to achieve in the world I had better be out of it. On the contrary, when I retired to rest after the receipt of Nikola's letter, as narrated in the preceding chapter, it was with a happier heart than I had known for more than two years past, and a fixed determination that, happen what might, even if his wonderful experiment came to naught, my new employer should not find me lacking in desire to serve him. As for that experiment itself, I scarcely knew what to think of it. To a man who had studied the human frame, its wonderful mechanism combined with its many deficiences and limitations, it seemed impossible it could succeed. And yet, strange as it may appear to say so, there was something about Nikola that made one feel sure he would not embark upon such an undertaking if he were not quite certain, or at least had not a well-grounded hope, of being able to bring it to a favourable issue. However, successful or unsuccessful, the fact remained that I was to be associated with him, and the very thought of such co-operation was sufficient to send the blood tingling through my veins with new life and strength.

During the two days that elapsed between my meeting with Nikola and the arrival of the vessel for which he had told me to be on the look-out, I saw nothing of Kelleran. I was not idle, however. In the first place it was necessary for me to replenish my wardrobe, which, as I have already observed, stood in need of considerable additions, and in the second I was anxious to consult some books of reference to which Nikola had directed my attention. By the time I had done these things, I had not, as may be supposed, very much leisure left, either for paying visits or for receiving them. I was careful, however, to write thanking him for the good turn he had done me, and wishing him good-bye in case I did not see him before I left.

5

"I inquired for the skipper."

It was between eight and nine o'clock on the Monday morning following that I received a note from the Steamship Company, to which Nikola had referred, advising me that their vessel the *Dona Mercedes* had arrived from Cadiz and was now lying in the river, and would sail for the North at eleven o'clock precisely. Accordingly I gathered my luggage together, what there was of it, and made my way down to her. As Nikola had predicted, I found her lying in the Pool.

On boarding her I was confronted by a big, burly man with a long brown beard, which blew over either shoulder and met behind his head as if it were some new kind of comforter. I inquired for the skipper.

"I am the captain," he answered. "And I suppose you are Dr. Ingleby. I had a letter from the owners saying you were going North with us. You may be sure we'll do our best to make you comfortable. In the meantime the steward will show you your berth and look after your luggage."

As he said this he beckoned a hand aft and sent him below in search of the official in question.

"I think you have a lady and gentleman on board who are expecting me?" I remarked, after the momentary pause which followed the man's departure.

"That I have, sir," he answered with emphasis; "and a nice responsibility they've been for me. I wouldn't undertake another like it if I were paid a hundred pounds extra for my trouble. But perhaps you know the old gentleman?"

"I have never seen him in my life," I replied, "but I have to take charge of him until we get to the North."

"Then I wish you joy of your work," he continued. "You'll have your time pretty fully occupied, I can tell you."

"In what way?" I inquired. "I shall consider it a favour if you will tell me all you can about him. Is the old gentleman eccentric, or what is the matter with him?"

"Eccentric?" replied the skipper, rolling his tongue round the word as if he liked its flavour, "Well, he may be that for all I know, but it's not his eccentricity that gives the trouble. It's his age! Why, I'll be bound he's a hundred, if he's a day. He's not a man at all, only a bag of bones; can't move out of his berth, can't walk, can't talk, and can't do a single hand's turn to help himself. His bones are almost through his skin, his eyes are sunk so far into his head that you can only guess what they're like, and when he wants a meal, or when he's got to have one, I should say, for he's past *wanting* anything, why, I'm blest if he hasn't to be fed with pap like a baby. It's a pitiful sort of a plight for a man to come to. What do you think? He'd far better be dead and buried."

I thought I understood. Putting one thing and another together, the reason of the old man's journey North could easily be guessed. At that moment the seaman, whom the skipper had sent in search of the steward, made his appearance from the companion, followed by the functionary in question. To the latter's charge I was consigned, and at his suggestion I followed him to the cabin which had been set aside for my accommodation. It proved to be situated at the after end of the saloon, and was as small and poorly furnished a place as I have ever slept in. To make use of the old nautical expression, there was scarcely room in it to swing a cat. Tiny as it was, however, it was at least better than the back street lodgings I had so lately left; and when I reflected that I had paid all I owed, had fitted myself out with a new wardrobe, and was still upwards of fifty pounds in pocket, to say nothing of being engaged on deeply interesting work, I could have gone down on my knees and kissed the grimy planks in thankfulness.

"I'm afraid, sir, it's not as large as some you've been accustomed to," said the talkative steward apologetically, as he stowed my bags away in a corner.

"How do you know what I've been accustomed to?" I asked, with a smile, as I noticed his desire for conversation.

"I could tell it directly I saw you look round this berth," he answered. "People can say what they please, but to my thinking there's no mistaking a man who's spent any time aboard ship. What line might you have been in, sir?"

I told him, and had the good fortune to discover that he possessed a brother who had served the same employ. Having thus established a bond in common, I proceeded to question him about my future charges; only to find that this was a subject upon which he was very willing to enlarge.

"Well, sir," he began, seating himself familiarly on the edge of my berth and looking up at me, "I don't know as how I ought to speak about the old gentleman at all, seeing he's a passenger and you're, so to speak, in charge of him; but this I do say without fear or favour, that who ever brought him away from his home and took him to sea at his time of life did a wrong and cruel action. Why, sir, I make so bold as to tell you that from the moment he was brought aboard this ship until this very second, he has not spoke as much as five words to me or to anybody else. He just lays there in his bunk, hour after hour, with his eyes open, looking at the deck above him, and as likely as not holding his great-granddaughter's hand, not seeming to see or hear anything, and never letting one single word pass his lips. I've known what it is to wait upon sick folk myself, having spent close upon eight months in a hospital ashore, but never in my life, sir, and I give you my word it's gospel truth I'm telling you, have I seen anything like the way that young girl waits upon him. You'll find her a-sitting by him after breakfast, and if you go in at eight bells she'll be still the same. She has her meals brought to her and eats 'em there, and at night she gets me to make her up a bed on the deck alongside of him."

"She must indeed be devoted," I answered, considerably touched at the picture he drew.

"Devoted is no name for it," replied the man with conviction. "And it's by no means pleasant work for her, sir, I can assure you. Why, more than once when I've gone in there I've found her leaning over the bunk, her face just as white as the sheet there, holding a little looking-glass to his lips to see if he was breathing. Then she'd heave a big sigh of relief to find that there was still life in him, put the glass back in its place, and sit down beside him again, and go on holding his hand, for all the world as if she was determined to cling on to him until the Judgment Day. It would bring the tears into your eyes, I'm sure, sir, to see it."

"You have a tender heart, I can see," I said, "and I think the better of you for it. Do you happen to know anything of their history—where they hail from or who they are?"

"There is one thing I *do* know," he answered, "and that is that they're English and not Spaniards, as the cook said, and as you might very well think yourself from the name. I believe the old gentleman was a merchant of some sort in Cadiz, but that must have been fifty years ago. The young lady is his great-granddaughter, and I was given to understand that her father and mother have been dead for many years. From one thing and another I don't fancy they've got a penny to bless themselves with, but it's plain there's somebody paying the piper, because the skipper got orders from the office, just before we sailed, that everything that could be done for their comfort was to be done, and money was to be no object. But there, here I am running on in this way to you, sir, who probably know all about them better than I do."

"I assure you I know nothing at all, or at least very little," I answered. "I have simply received instructions to meet them here, and to look after the old gentleman until he reaches Newcastle. What will become of them then I can only guess. I presume, however, I may rely on you for assistance during the voyage, should I require it?"

"I'll do anything I can, sir, and you may be very sure of that," he replied. "I've taken such a liking to that young lady that there's nothing I wouldn't do in reason to make her feel a bit happier. For it's my belief she's far from easy in her mind just now. I remember once hearing an Orient steward tell of a man what was tied up with a sword hanging over his head by a single hair; he never knew from one minute to another when it would fall and do for him. Well, that's the way, I fancy, Miss Moreno is feeling. There's a sword hanging over her head or her great-grandfather's, and she doesn't know when it'll drop."

"What did you say her name was?" I inquired, for I had for the moment forgotten it.

"Moreno, sir," he replied. "The old gentleman is Don Miguel, and she is the Dona Consuelo de Moreno."

"Thank you," I said. "And now, if you will tell me where their cabin is, I think I will pay the old gentleman a visit."

"Their cabin is the one facing yours, sir, on the starboard side. If it will be any convenience to you, sir, I'll tell the young lady you're aboard. I know she expects you, because she said so only this morning."

"Perhaps it would be better that you should tell her," I replied. "If you will give her my compliments and say that I will do myself the pleasure of waiting upon her as soon as it is convenient for her to see me, I shall be obliged. I will remain here until I receive her answer."

The man departed on his errand, and during his absence I spent the time making myself as comfortable as my limited quarters would permit. It was not very long, however, before he returned to inform me that the young lady would be pleased to see me as soon as I cared to visit their cabin.

Placing my stethoscope in my pocket, and having thrown a hasty glance into the small looking-glass over the washstand, in order to make sure that I presented a fairly respectable appearance, I left my quarters and made my way across the saloon. Since then I have often tried to recall my feelings at that moment, but the effort has always been in vain. One thing is certain, I had no idea of the importance the incident was destined to occupy in the history of my life.

I knocked upon the door, and as I did so heard some one rise from a chair inside the cabin. The handle was softly turned, and a moment later the most beautiful girl I have ever seen in my life stood before me. I have said "the most beautiful girl," but this does not at all express what I mean, nor do I think it is in my power to do so. Let me, however, endeavour to give you some idea of what Dona Consuelo de Moreno was like.

Try to picture a tall and stately girl, in reality scarcely twenty years of age, but looking several years older. Imagine a pale, oval face, lighted by dark lustrous eyes with long lashes and delicately pencilled brows, a tiny mouth, and hair as black as the raven's wing. Taken altogether, it was not only a very beautiful face, but a strong one, and as I looked at her I wondered what the circumstances could have been that had brought her into the power of my extraordinary employer. That she was in his power I did not for a moment doubt.

Closing the cabin door softly behind her, she stepped into the saloon.

"The steward tells me that you are Dr. Ingleby," she began, speaking excellent English, but with a slight foreign accent. Then, holding out her tiny hand to me with charming frankness, she continued: "I was informed by Dr. Nikola, in a letter I received this morning, that you would join the vessel here. It is a great relief to me to know you are on board."

I said something, I forget what, in answer to the compliment she paid me, and then inquired how her aged relative was.

"He seems fairly well at present," she answered. "As well, perhaps, as he will ever be. But, as you may suppose, he has given me a great deal of anxiety since we left Cadiz. This vessel is not a good sea boat, and in the Bay of Biscay we had some very rough weather—so rough, indeed, that more than once I thought she must inevitably founder. However, we are safely here now, so that our troubles are nearly over. I don't want you to think I am a grumbler. But I am keeping you here when perhaps you would like to see grandpapa for yourself?"

I answered in the affirmative, whereupon she softly opened the door again, and, beckoning me to follow, led the way into the cabin.

If my own quarters on the other side of the saloon had seemed small, this one seemed even smaller. There was only one bunk, and it ran below the port-hole. In this an old man was lying with his hands clasped upon his breast.

"You need not fear that you will wake him," said the girl beside me. "He sleeps like this the greater part of the day. Sometimes he frightens me, for he lies so still that I become afraid lest he may have passed away without my noticing it."

I did not at all wonder at her words. The old man's pallor was of that peculiar ivory-white which is never seen save in the very old, and then, strangely enough, in men oftener than women. His eyes were deeply sunken, as were his cheeks. At one time—forty years or so before—it must have been a powerful face; now it was beautiful only in its soft, harmonious whiteness. A long beard, white as the purest snow, fell upon, and covered his breast, and on it lay his fleshless hands, with their bony joints and long yellow nails. The better to examine him, I knelt down beside the bunk and took his right wrist between my finger and thumb. As I expected, the pulse was barely perceptible. For a moment I inclined to the belief that the end, of which his great-granddaughter had spoken only a few moments before, had come, but a second examination proved that such was not the case. I gently replaced his hand, and then rose to my feet.

"I can easily understand your anxiety," I said. "I think you are wonderfully brave to have undertaken such a voyage. However, for the future—that is to say, until we reach Newcastle—you must let me share your watch with you."

"It is very kind of you to offer to do so," she replied, "but I could not remain away from him. I have had charge of him for such a long time now that it has become like second nature to me. Besides, if he were to wake and not find me by his side, there is no saying what might happen. I am everything to him, and I know so well what he requires."

As she said this, she gave me a look that I could not help thinking was almost one of defiance, as if she were afraid that by attending to the old man's wants I might deprive her of his affection. I accordingly postponed consideration of the matter for the moment, and, having asked a few questions as to the patient's diet, retired, leaving them once more alone together. From the saloon I made my way up to the poop. The tide was serving, and preparations were being made for getting under way.

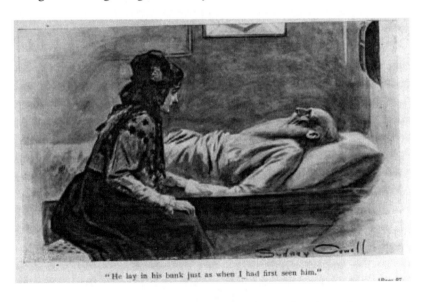

"He lay in his bunk just as when I had first seen him."

Ten minutes later our anchor was at the cathead, and we were steaming slowly down the river, and I had begun one of the most extraordinary voyages it has ever fallen to the lot of man to undertake. During the afternoon I paid several visits to my patient's cabin; but on no occasion could I discover any change in his condition. He lay in his bunk just as I had first seen him; his sunken eyes stared at the woodwork above his head, and his left hand clasped that of his great-granddaughter. To my surprise, the motion of the vessel seemed to cause him little or no inconvenience, and, fortunately for him, his nurse was an excellent sailor. It was in vain I tried to induce her to let me take her place while she went up to the deck for a little change. Her grandfather might want her, she said, and that excuse seemed to her sufficient to justify such trifling with her health. Later on, however, after dinner, I was fortunate enough to be able to induce her to accompany me to the deck for a few moments, the steward being left in charge of the patient, with instructions to call us should the least change occur. By this time we were clear of the river, and our bows were pointed in a northerly direction. Leaving the miserable companion, which ascended to the poop directly from the cuddy, we began to pace the deck. The night was cold, and, with a little shiver, my companion drew her coquettish mantilla more closely about her shoulders. There was something in her action which touched me in a manner I cannot describe. In some vague fashion it seemed to appeal to me not only for sympathy but for help. I saw the beautiful face looking up at me, and as we walked I noted the proud way in which she carried herself, and the sailor-like fashion in which she adapted herself to the rolling of the ship. It was a beautiful moonlight night, and had the vessel remained upon an even keel, it would have been very pleasant on deck. To be steady, however, was a feat the crazy old tub seemed incapable of accomplishing.

We had paced the poop perhaps half a dozen times when my companion suddenly stopped, and placing her hand upon my arm, said:

"Dr. Ingleby, you are in Dr. Nikola's confidence, I believe. Will you tell me why we are going to the North of England?"

Her question placed me in an awkward predicament. As I have said above, her loneliness, not to mention the devotion she showed to her aged relative, had touched me more than a little. On the other hand, I was Nikola's servant, employed by him for a special work, and I did not know whether he would wish me to discuss his plans with her.

" 'Dr. Ingleby, you are in Dr. Nikola's confidence, I believe.'

"You do not answer," she continued, as she noticed my hesitation. "And yet I feel sure you must know. It all seems so strange. Only a few weeks ago we were in our own quiet home in Spain, without a thought of leaving it. Then Dr. Nikola came upon the scene, and now we are on board this ship going up to the North of England: and for what purpose?"

"Did Nikola furnish you with no reason?" I inquired.

"Oh yes," she replied. "He told me that if I would bring my grandfather to England to see him he would make him quite a strong man again. For some reason or another, however, I feel certain there is something behind it that is being kept from me. Is this so?"

"I am not in a position to give you any answer that would be at all likely to satisfy you," I replied, I am afraid, a little ambiguously, "for I really know nothing. It is only fair I should tell you that I only met Dr. Nikola, myself, for the first time a few days ago."

"But he sent you here to be with my grandfather," she continued authoritatively. "Surely, Dr. Ingleby, you must be able to throw some light upon the mystery which surrounds this voyage?"

I shook my head, and with a little sigh of regret she ceased to question me. A few minutes later she gave me a stately bow, and, bidding me goodnight, prepared to go below. Knowing that I had deceived her, and hoping to find some opportunity of putting myself right with her, I followed her down the companion-ladder and along the saloon to her cabin.

"Perhaps I had better see my patient before I retire to rest," I said, as we stood together at the door, holding on to the handrail and balancing ourselves against the rolling of the ship.

She threw a quick glance at me, as if for some reason she were surprised at my decision; the expression, however, passed from her face as quickly as it had come, and opening the door she entered the cabin, and I followed her. She could scarcely have advanced a step towards the bunk before she uttered an exclamation of surprise and horror. The steward, who was supposed to have been watching the invalid, was fast asleep, while the latter's head had slipped from its pillow and was now lying in a most unnatural position, his chin in the air, his eyes open, but still fixed upon the ceiling in the same glassy stare I have described before. In her dismay the girl said something in Spanish which I am unable to interpret, and leaning over the bunk, gazed into her great-grandfather's face as if she were afraid of what she might find there. The steward meanwhile had recovered his senses, and was staring stupidly from one to the other of us, hardly able to realise the consequences of his inattention. Though all this has taken some time to describe it was in reality the action of a moment; then signing to the steward to stand back, and gently pushing the young girl to one side, I knelt down and commenced my examination of my patient. There could be no doubt about one thing, the old man's condition was eminently serious. If he lived at all, there was but little more than a flicker of life left in him. How to preserve that flicker was a question that at first glance appeared impossible to answer. It would have been better, and certainly kinder, to have let him go in peace. This, however, I was in honour bound not to do. He was Nikola's property, whose servant I also was, and if it were possible to keep him alive I knew I must do it.

"Oh, Dr. Ingleby, surely he cannot be dead?" cried the girl behind me, in a voice that had grown hoarse with fear. "Tell me the worst, I implore you."

"Hush!" I answered, but without looking round. "You must be brave. He is not dead. Nor will he die if I can save him."

Then turning to the steward, who was still with us, I bade him hasten to my cabin and bring me the small bag he would find hanging upon the peg behind the door. When he returned with it I took from it one of the small bottles it contained, the contents of which I had been directed by Nikola to use only in the event of the case seeming absolutely hopeless. The mixture was tasteless, odourless, and quite colourless, and of a liquidity equal to water. I poured the stipulated quantity into a spoon and forced it between the old man's lips. Somewhat to my surprise—for I must confess, after what I had seen of Nikola's power a few nights before, I had expected an instantaneous cure—the effect was scarcely perceptible. The eyelids flickered a little, and then slowly closed; a few seconds later a respiratory movement of the thorax was just observable, accompanied by a heavy sigh. For upwards of an hour I remained in close attendance upon him, noting every symptom, and watching with amazement the return of life into that aged frame from which I had begun to think it had departed for good and all. Once more I measured the quantity of medicine and gave it to him. This time the effect was more marked. At the end of ten minutes a slight flush spread over the sunken cheeks, and his breathing could be plainly distinguished. When, after the third dose, he was sleeping peacefully as a little child, I turned to the girl and held out my hand.

"He will recover," I said. "You need have no further fear. The crisis is past."

She was silent for a moment, and I noticed that her eyes had filled with tears.

"You have done *a* most wonderful thing," she answered, "and have punished me for my rudeness to you on deck. How can I ever thank you?"

"By ceasing to give me credit to which I am not entitled," I replied, I fear a little brusquely. "This medicine comes from Dr. Nikola, and I think should be as good a proof as you can desire of the genuineness of his offer and of his ability to make your grandfather a strong and hearty man again."

"I will not doubt him any more," she said: and after that, having made her promise to call me should she need my services, I bade her good' night and left the cabin, meaning to retire to rest at once. The stuffiness of my berth, however, changed my intention. After all that had transpired, it can scarcely be wondered at that I was in a state of feverish excitement. In love with my profession as I was, it will be readily understood that I had sufficient matter before me to afford plenty of food for reflection. I accordingly filled my pipe and made my way to the deck. Once there, I found that the appearance of the night had changed; the moonlight had given place to heavy clouds, and rain was falling. The steamer was still rolling heavily, and every timber groaned as if in protest against the barbarous handling to which it was being subjected. Stowing myself away in a sheltered place near the alley-way leading to the engine-room, I fell to considering my position. That it was a curious one, I do not think any one who has read the preceding pages will doubt. A more extraordinary could scarcely be imagined, and what the upshot of it all was to be was a thing I could not at all foresee.

Having finished my pipe, I refilled it and continued my meditations. At a rough guess, I should say I had been an hour on deck when a circumstance occurred which was destined to furnish me with even more food for reflection than I already possessed. I was in the act of knocking the ashes out of my pipe before going below, when I became aware that something, I could not quite see what, was making its way along the deck in my direction under the shadow of the starboard bulwark. At first I felt inclined to believe that it was only a trick of my imagination, but when I rubbed my eyes and saw that it was a human figure, and that it was steadily approaching me, I drew back into the shadow and awaited developments. From the stealthy way in which he advanced, and the trouble he took to prevent himself being seen, I argued that, whoever the man was, and whatever his mission might be, it was not a very reputable one. Closer and closer he came, was lost to view for an instant behind the mainmast, and then reappeared scarcely a dozen feet from where I stood. For a moment I hardly knew what course to adopt. I had no desire to rouse the ship unnecessarily, and yet, for the reasons just stated, I felt morally certain that the man was there for no lawful purpose. However, if I was going to act at all, it was plain I must do so without loss of time. Fortune favoured me, for I had scarcely arrived at this decision before the chief engineer, whose cabin looked out over the deck, turned on his electric light. A broad beam of light shot out and showed me the man standing beside the main hatch steadfastly regarding me. Before he could move I was able to take full stock of him, and what I saw filled me with amazement. *The individual was a Chinaman, and his head presented this peculiarity, that half his left ear was missing.*

As I noted the significant fact to which I have just alluded, the recollection of Nikola's letter flashed across my mind, in which he had warned me to keep my eyes open for just such another man. Could this be the individual for whom I was to be on the look-out? It seemed extremely unlikely that there could be two Mongolians with the same peculiar deformity, and yet I could scarcely believe, even if it were the same and he had any knowledge of my connection with Nikola, that he would have the audacity to travel in the same ship with me. It must not be supposed, however, that I stayed to think these things out then. The light had no sooner flashed out upon him and revealed his sinister personality, than the switch was turned off and all was darkness once more. So blinding was the glare while it did last, however, that fully ten seconds must have elapsed before my eyes became accustomed to the darkness. When I could see, the man had vanished, and though I crossed the hatch and searched, not a sign of him could I discover.

"Whoever he is," I said to myself, "he has at least the faculty of being able to get out of the way pretty quickly. I wonder what . . . but there, what's the use of worrying myself about him? He's probably a fireman who has been sent aft on a message to the steward, and when I see him in the daylight I shall find him like anybody else."

But while I tried to reassure myself in this fashion I was in reality far from being convinced. In my own mind I was as certain that he was the man against whom Nikola had warned me as I could well be of anything. The chief engineer at that moment stepped from his cabin into the alley-way. Here, I thought to myself, was an opportunity of settling the matter once and for all. I accordingly accosted him. I had been introduced to him earlier in the day by the captain, so that he knew who I was.

"Could this be the individual of whom I had to beware?"

"That is not a very pretty fireman of yours," I began, "that Chinaman with half an ear missing. I saw him a moment ago coming along the deck here. Where does he hail from?"

The chief engineer, who, I may remark *en passant*, was an Aberdonian, and consequently slow of speech, hesitated for a moment before he replied.

"That's mighty queer," he said at length. "Ye're the second mon who's seen him the night. D'ye tell me ye saw him this meenit? And if I may make so bold, where might that have been?"

"Only a few paces from where we are standing now," I answered. "I was smoking my pipe in the shelter there, when suddenly I detected a figure creeping along in the shadow of the bulwarks. Then you turned on your electric, and the light fell full and fair upon his face. I saw him perfectly. There could be no doubt about it. He was a Chinaman, and half his left ear was missing."

The chief engineer sucked at his pipe for upwards of half a minute.

"Queer, queer," he said, more to himself than to me, "'tis vera queer. 'Twas my second in yonder was saying he met him at eight bells in this alley-way. And yet I've been officially acquented there's no such person aboard the ship."

"But there must be," I cried. "Don't I tell you I saw the man myself, not five minutes ago? I would be willing to go into a court of law and swear to the fact."

"Dinna swear," he answered. "I'll nae misdoubt yer word."

With this assurance I was conducted forthwith to the chart room, where we discovered the skipper stretched upon his settee, snoring voluminously.

"Do you mean to tell me that you really saw the man?" he inquired, when my business had been explained to him.

I assured him that I did mean it. I had seen him distinctly.

"Well, all I can say is that it's the most extraordinary business I ever had to do with," he answered. "The second engineer also says he saw him. Directly he told me I had the ship searched, but not a trace of the fellow could I discover. We'll try again."

Leaving the chart room, he called the bos'un to him, and, accompanied by the chief engineer and myself, commenced an exhaustive examination of the vessel. We explored the quarters of the crew and firemen forrard, the galley, stores, and officers' cabins in both alley-ways, and finally the saloon aft, but without success. Not a trace of the mysterious Mongolian could we find. The skipper shook his head.

"I don't know what to think about it," he said.

I knew that meant that he had his doubts as to whether I had not dreamt the whole affair. The inference was galling, and when I bade him goodnight and went along to my cabin, I wished I had said nothing at all about the matter. Nevertheless, I was as firmly convinced that I had seen the man as I was at the beginning. In this frame of mind I prepared myself for bed. Before turning into my bunk, however, I took down the small bag in which I kept the drugs Nikola had given me and of which he had told me to take such care. I was anxious to have them close at hand in case I should be sent for by Dona Consuelo during the night. To assure myself that they had not been broken by the rolling of the ship I opened the bag and looked inside. My astonishment may be imagined on discovering that it was empty. *The drugs were gone.*

CHAPTER IV. THE CHINAMAN'S ESCAPE

THE night on which I discovered that Nikola's drugs had been stolen was destined to prove unpleasant in more senses than one. The sweetest-tempered of men could scarcely have failed to take offence had they been treated as the captain had treated me. I had told him in so many words, and with as much emphasis as I was master of, that I had distinctly seen the Chinaman standing upon the main deck of his steamer. The second engineer had also entered the same report; his evidence, however, while serving to corroborate my assertion, was of little further use to me, inasmuch as I had still better proof that what I said was correct—namely, that the medicines were missing. Under the circumstances it was small wonder that I slept badly. Even had the cabin been as large as a hotel bedroom, and the bunk the latest invention in the way of comfortable couches, it is scarcely possible I should have had better rest. As it was, the knowledge that I had been outwitted was sufficient to keep me tumbling and tossing to and fro, from the moment I laid my head upon the pillow until the sun was streaming in through my porthole next morning. Again and again I went over the events of the previous day, recalling every incident with photographic distinctness; but always returning to the same point. How the man could have obtained admittance to the saloon at all was more than I could understand, and, having got there, why he should have stolen the bottles of medicine when there were so many other articles which would have seemed to be of infinitely more value to him, scattered about, was, to say the least of it, incomprehensible. Hour after hour I puzzled over it, and at the end was no nearer a solution of the enigma than at the beginning. At first I felt inclined to believe that I must have taken them from the bag myself and for security's sake have placed them elsewhere. A few moments' search, however, was sufficient to knock the bottom out of that theory. Hunt high and low, where I would, I could discover no traces of the queer little bottles. Then I remembered that when I had sent the steward for them to the Don's cabin the previous afternoon, I had taken them from the bag and placed them upon the deck beside the old man's bunk. Could I have left them there? On reconsidering the matter more carefully, however, I remembered that before leaving the cabin I had replaced them in my bag, and that as I carried them back to my berth I had bumped the satchel against the corner of the saloon table and was afraid I might have broken them. This effectually disposed of that theory also. At last the suspense of irritation, by whichever name you may describe it, became unbearable, and unable to remain in bed any longer, I rose, dressed myself, and prepared to go on deck. Entering the saloon, I found the steward busied over a number of coffee-cups.

"Good morning, sir," he said, looking up from his work. "If you'll excuse my saying so, sir, you're about early."

"I was late in bed," I answered, with peculiar significance. "How is it, my friend, that you allow people, who have no right here, to enter the saloon and to thieve from the passengers' cabins?"

"To thieve, sir!" the man replied in a startled tone; "I'm sure I don't understand you, sir. I allow no one to enter the saloon who has no right to *be* there."

I glanced at him sharply, wondering whether the fellow was as innocent as he pretended to be.

"At any rate," I said, "the fact remains that some one entered my cabin last night, while I was on deck, and stole the medicines with which I am treating the old gentleman in the cabin yonder."

The man looked inexpressibly shocked. "God bless my soul alive, sir—you don't mean that!" he said, with a falter in his voice. "Surely you don't mean it?"

"But I *do* mean it," I answered. "There can be no sort of doubt about it. When I left the old gentleman's cabin yesterday I carried the bag containing the medicines back with me to my own berth, locked it, and hung it upon the peg beside the looking-glass with my own hands. After that I went on deck, returned to my cabin an hour or so later, opened the bag, and the bottles were gone."

"But, sir, have you any idea who could have taken them?" the man replied. "I hope you don't think, sir, as how I should have allowed such a thing to take place in this saloon with my knowledge?"

"I hope you would not," I answered, "but that does not alter the fact that the things are missing."

"But don't you think, sir, the young lady herself might have come in search of you, and when she found you were not there did the next best thing and took away the medicines to use herself?"

"At present I do not know what to think," I replied with some hesitation, for that view of the case had not presented itself to me. "But if there has been anything underhand going on, I think I can promise the culprit that it will be made exceedingly hot for him when we reach our destination."

Having fired this parting shot, I left him to the contemplation of his coffee-cups and made my way up the companion-ladder to the deck above. It was a lovely morning, a brisk breeze was blowing, and the steamer was running fairly steady under a staysail and a foresail. It was not the sort of morning to feel depressed, and yet the incidents of the previous night were sufficient to render me more than a little uncomfortable. Nikola had trusted me, and in the matter of the medicines at least I had been found wanting. I believe at the moment I would have given all I possessed—which was certainly not much, but still a good deal to me—to have been able to solve the mystery that surrounded the disappearance of those drugs. Shortly before eight bells the skipper emerged from the chart room and came along the hurricane deck towards the poop. Seeing me he waved his hand, and, after he had ascended the ladder from the main deck, bade me good morning. "I'm afraid our accommodation is not very good," he said, "but I trust you have passed a fairly comfortable night. No more dreams of one-eared Chinamen, I hope?"

From the tone in which he spoke it was plain that he imagined I must have been dreaming on the previous evening. Had it not been for the seriousness of my position with Nikola, I could have laughed aloud when I thought of the shell I was about to drop into the skipper's camp.

"Dreams or no dreams, Captain Windover," I replied, "I have to make a very serious complaint to you. It will remain then for you to say whether you consider that the assertion I made to you last night was, or was not, founded upon fact. As I believe you are aware, I was instructed by my principal, Dr. Nikola, to join this vessel in the Thames and to take charge of Don Miguel de Moreno until his arrival in Newcastle-on-Tyne. Dr. Nikola was fully aware of the difficulty and responsibility of the task he had assigned to me, and for this reason he furnished me with a number of very rare drugs which I was to administer to the patient as occasion demanded. In the letter of instructions which I received prior to embarking, I was particularly warned to beware of a certain Chinaman whose peculiar characteristic was that he had lost half an ear. In due course I joined your vessel, and attended the Don, used the drugs to which I have referred, and afterwards returned them to my cabin. A quarter of an hour or so later I made my way to the deck, where I found myself suddenly brought face to face with the Asiatic of whom I had been warned. On the recommendation of the chief engineer I reported the matter to you; you searched the ship, found no one at all like the man I described, and from that time forward set down the story I had told you either as a fabrication on my part, or the creation of a dream."

"Pardon me, my dear sir, not a fabrication," the skipper began: "only a—"

"Pardon me in your turn," I replied: "I have not quite finished. As I have inferred, you treat the matter with contempt. What *is* the result? I return to my cabin, and, before retiring to rest, in order to make sure that they are ready at hand in case I should require them during the night, open the bag in which the medicines until that moment had been stored. To my consternation they are not there. Some one had entered my cabin during my absence and stolen them. I leave you to put what construction on it you please, and to say what that some one was."

64

The captain's face was a study. "But&mdash but—" he began.

"Buts will not mend the matter," I answered, I am afraid rather sharply. "There can be no getting away from the fact that they are gone, and that some one must have taken them. They could scarcely walk away by themselves."

"But supposing your suspicions to be correct, what possible use could a few small bottles of unknown medicine be to a man like that, a Chinaman? Had he taken your watch and chain, or your money, I could understand it; but from what you say, I gather that nothing else is missing."

"Nothing else," I replied, in the tone of a man who is making an admission that is scarcely likely to add to the weight of the argument he is endeavouring to adduce.

"Besides," continued the skipper, "there are half a hundred other ways in which the things might have been lost or mislaid. Last night the ship was rolling heavily: why might they not have tumbled out and have slipped under your bunk or behind your bags? I have known things like that occur."

"And would the ship have closed the bag again, may I ask?" I answered scornfully. "No, no! Captain, I am afraid that won't do. The man I reported to you last night, the one-eared Chinaman, is aboard your ship, and for some reason best known to himself he has stolen some of my property, thereby not only inconveniencing me but placing in absolute danger the life of the old man whom I was sent on board to take care of. As the thief is scarcely likely to have jumped overboard, he must be on board now; and as he would not be likely to have stolen the bottles only to smash them, it stands to reason that he must have them in his keeping at the present moment."

"And suppose he has, what do you want me to do?"

"I want you to find him for me," I answered, "or, if you don't care to take the trouble, to put sufficient men at my disposal and allow me to do so."

On hearing this the captain became very red and shifted uneasily on his feet.

"My dear sir," he said a little testily, "much as I would like to put myself out to serve you, I must confess that what you ask seems a little unreasonable. Don't I tell you I have already searched the ship twice in an attempt to find this man, and each time without success? Upon my word I don't think it is fair to ask me to do so again."

"In that case I am very much afraid I have no alternative but to make a complaint to you in writing and to hold you responsible, should Don Miguel de Moreno lose his life through this robbery which has been committed, and which you will not help me to set right."

What the captain would have answered in reply to this I cannot say; it is quite certain, however, that it would have been something sharp had not the Dofia Consuelo made her appearance from the companion hatch that moment. She struck me as looking very pale, as if she had passed a bad night. The skipper and I went forward together to meet her.

"Good morning," I said, as I took the little hand she held out to me. "I hope your great-grandfather is better this morning?"

"He has passed a fairly good-night, and is sleeping quietly at present," she answered. "The steward is sitting with him now while I come up for a few moments to get a little fresh air on deck."

The skipper made some remark about the beauty of the morning, and while he was speaking I watched the girl's face. There was an expression upon it I did not quite understand.

"I am afraid you have not passed a very good-night," I said, after the other had finished. "Yesterday's anxiety must have upset you more than you allowed me to suppose."

"I will confess that it did upset me," she answered, with her pretty foreign accent and the expressive gesticulation which was so becoming to her. "I have had a wretched night. I had such a terrible dream that I have scarcely recovered from it yet."

"I am sorry to hear that," the skipper and I answered almost together, while I added, "Pray tell us about it."

"It does not seem very much to tell," she answered, "and yet the effect it produced upon me is just as vivid now as it was then. After you left the cabin last night, Dr. Ingleby, I sat for a little while by my grandfather's side, trying to read; but finding that impossible, I retired to rest, lying upon the bed the steward is kind enough to make up for me upon the floor. I was utterly worn out, and almost as soon as I closed my eyes I fell asleep. How long I had been sleeping I cannot say, but suddenly I felt there was some one in the room who was watching me: who it was I could not tell, but that it was some one, or something, utterly repulsive to me I felt certain. In vain I endeavoured to open my eyes, but, as in most nightmares, I found it impossible to do so; and all the time I could feel this loathsome thing, whatever it was, drawing closer and closer to me. Then, putting forth a great effort, I managed to wake, or perhaps to dream that I did so. I had much better have kept my eyes closed, for leaning over me was the most horrible face I have ever seen or imagined. It was flatter than that of a European, with small, narrow eyes, and such cruel eyes."

"Good heavens!" I cried, unable to keep silence any longer, "can it be possible that you saw him too?"

Meanwhile the skipper, who had been leaning against the bulwarks, his hands thrust deep in his pockets and his cap upon the back of his head, suddenly sprang to attention.

"Can you remember anything else about the man?" he inquired.

The girl considered for a moment.

"I do not know that I can," she answered. "I can only repeat what I said before, that it was the most awful face I have ever seen in my life.—Stay, there is one other thing that I remember. I noticed that half his left ear was missing."

"It is the Chinaman!" I cried, with an air of triumph that I could no longer suppress. And as I said it I took from my pocket the letter of instruction Nikola had sent me the week before, and read aloud the passage in which he referred to the one-eared Chinaman of whom I was to beware. The effect was exactly what I imagined it would be.

"Do you mean to tell me I was not dreaming after all?" the Dona inquired, with a frightened expression on her face.

"That is exactly what I *do* mean," I answered. "And I am glad to have your evidence that you saw the man, for the reason that it bears out what I have been saying to our friend the captain here."

Then turning to that individual, I continued: "I hope, sir, you will now see the advisability of instituting another search for this man. If I were in your place I would turn the ship inside out, from truck to keelson. It seems to me outrageous that a rascal like this can hide himself on board, and you, the captain, be ignorant of his whereabouts."

"There is no necessity to instruct me in my duty," he answered stiffly, and then going to the companion called down it for the steward, who presently made his appearance on deck.

"Williams," said the skipper, "Dr. Ingleby informs me that a theft was committed in his cabin last night. He declares that a man made his way into the saloon, visiting not only his berth, but that of Don Miguel de Moreno. How do you account for this?"

"Dr. Ingleby *did* say something to me about it this morning, sir," the steward replied: "but to tell you the plain truth, sir, I don't know what to think of it. It's the first time I've ever known such a thing happen. Of course I shouldn't like to say as how Dr. Ingleby was mistaken."

"You had better not," I replied, so sharply that the man jumped with surprise.

"Anyway, sir," the steward continued, "I feel certain that if the man *had* come aft I should have heard him. I am a light sleeper, as the saying is, and I believe that a cat coming down the companion-ladder would be enough to wake me, much less a man."

"On this occasion you must have slept sounder than usual," I said. "At any rate the fact remains that the man did come; and I have to ask you once more, Captain, what you intend to do to find my stolen property?"

"I must take time to consider the matter," the captain replied. "If the man is aboard the ship, as you assert, I will find him, and if I do find him he had better look out for squalls—that's all I can say."

"And at the same time," I added, "I hope you will severely punish any member of your crew who may have been instrumental in secreting him on board."

As I said this I glanced at the steward, and it seemed to me his always sallow face became even paler than usual.

"You need not bother yourself about that," said the skipper: "you may be sure I shall do so."

Then, lifting his cap to the Dona Consuelo, he went forward along the deck; while the steward, having informed us that breakfast was upon the table, returned to the companion-ladder and disappeared below.

"What does all this mystery mean, Dr. Ingleby?" inquired my companion, as we turned and walked aft together.

"It means that there is more at the back of it than meets the eye," I replied. "Before I left London I was warned by Dr. Nikola, as you heard me say just now, to beware of a certain Asiatic with only half an ear. What Nikola feared he would do I have no notion, but there seems to be no doubt that this is the man."

"But he has done us no harm," she replied, "beyond frightening me; so if the captain takes care that he does not come as far as the saloon again, it does not seem to me we need think any more about him."

"But he *has* done us harm," I asserted—"grievous harm. He has stolen the medicine with which I treated your great-grandfather so successfully yesterday."

On hearing this she gave a little start.

"Do you mean that if he should become ill again in the same way that he did yesterday, you would be unable to save him?" she inquired, almost breathlessly.

"I cannot say anything about that," I answered. "I should of course do my best, but I must confess the loss of those drugs is a very serious matter for me. They are exceedingly valuable, and were specially entrusted to my care."

"And you think that Dr. Nikola will be angry with you for having lost them?" she said.

"I am very much afraid he will," I answered. "But if he is, I must put up with it. Now let us come below to breakfast." With that I led her along the deck and down the companion-ladder to the saloon.

"Before we sit down to our meal I think it would perhaps be as well if I saw your great-grandfather," I said. "I should like to convince myself that he is none the worse for his attack yesterday."

70

Upon this we entered the cabin together, and I bent over the recumbent figure of the old man. He lay just as he had done on the previous day; his long thin hands were clasped upon his breast, and his eyes looked upward just as I remembered seeing them. For all the difference that was to be seen, he might never have moved since I had left him so many hours before.

"He is awake," whispered his great-granddaughter, who had looked at him over my shoulder. Then, raising her voice a little, she continued, still in English, "This is Dr. Ingleby, grandfather, whom your friend Dr. Nikola has sent to take care of you."

"I thank you, sir, for your kindness," replied the old man, in a voice that was little louder than a whisper. "You must forgive me if my reception of you appears somewhat discourteous, but I am very feeble. A month ago I celebrated my ninety-eighth birthday, and at such an age, I venture to assert, much may be forgiven a man."

"Pray do not apologise," I replied. "I am indeed glad to find you looking so much better this morning."

"If to be still alive is to be better, then I suppose I must be," he answered, in a tone that was almost one of regret; and then continued, "The days of our age are threescore years and ten; and though men be so strong that they come to fourscore years, yet is their strength but labour and sorrow; labour and sorrow—aye, labour and sorrow."

"Come, come, sir," I said, "you must not talk like this. You are not very comfortable here, but we are nearly at our journey's end. Once there, you will be able to rest more quietly and in greater comfort than it is possible for you to do in this tiny cabin."

"You speak well," he answered, "when you say that I am nearly at my journey's end." [section missing?]

God knows at least a dozen small boats; and thinking Nikola might be in one of them, I went forward to the gangway in search of him, but though I scanned the faces below me, his was not among them. For the reason that we were so late getting into the river, and knowing that the vessel would be likely to remain for some time to come, I argued that in all probability he had put off boarding her until the morning. I accordingly turned away, and was about to walk aft when a hand was placed on my shoulder.

"Well, friend Ingleby," said a voice that there was no mistaking, and which I should have known anywhere, "what sort of a voyage have you had, and how is your patient progressing?"

"Dr. Nikola!" I cried in astonishment, as I turned and found him standing before me. "I was just looking for you in the boats alongside. I had no idea you were on board."

"I came up by the other gangway," Nikola replied. "But you have not answered my question. How is your patient?"

"He is still alive," I answered, "and I fancy, if possible, a little better than when we left London. But he is so feeble that to speak of his being well seems almost a sarcasm. Yesterday for a few moments I thought he was gone, but with the help of the drugs you gave me I managed to bring him round again. This morning he was strong enough to converse with me."

"I am pleased to hear it," he replied. "You have done admirably, and I congratulate you. Now we must think about their trans-shipment."

"Trans-shipment?" I replied. "Is it possible they have to make another journey?"

"It is more than possible—it is quite certain," he answered. "Allerdeyne Castle is a matter of some fifty miles up the coast, and a steam yacht will take us there. A bed has been prepared for the old gentleman in the saloon, and all we have to do is to get him off this boat and on board her. You had better let me have those drugs and I'll mix him up a slight stimulus. He'll need it."

72

" To my amazement he was a Chinaman."

This was the question I had been dreading all along, but the die was cast and willy nilly the position had to be faced.

"I should like to speak to you upon that matter," I said. "I very much fear that you will consider me to blame for not having exercised greater care over them, but I had no idea they would be of any value to any one who did not know the use of them."

"Pray what do you mean?" he asked, with a look of astonishment that I believe was more than half assumed. "To what are you alluding? Have you had an accident with the drugs?"

While we had been talking we had walked along the main deck, and were approaching the entrance leading therefrom to the cuddy, the light from which fell upon his face. There was a look upon it that I did not like. When he was in an affable mood Nikola's countenance was singularly prepossessing: when, however, he was put out by anything it was the face of a devil rather than a man.

"I exceedingly regret having to inform you that last night the drugs in question were stolen from my cabin."

In a moment he was all excitement.

"By the man of whom I bade you beware, of course—the one-eared Chinaman?"

"The same," I answered; and went on to inform him of all that had transpired since my arrival on board, including my trouble with the captain and the suspicions I entertained, without much foundation I'm afraid, against the steward. He heard me out without speaking, and when I had finished bade me wait on deck while he went below to the Morenos' cabin. While he was gone I strolled to the side, and once more stood watching the lights reflected in the water below. On an old tramp steamer a short distance astern of us a man was singing. It was one of Chevalier's coster songs, and I could recognise the words quite distinctly. The last time I had heard that song was in Cape Coast Castle, just after I had recovered from my attack of fever;

and I was still pursuing the train of thought it conjured up, when I noticed a boat drawing into the circle of light to which I have just alluded. It contained two men, one of whom was standing up while the other rowed. A second or two later they had come close enough for me to see the face of the man in the bows. To my amazement he was a Chinaman! So overwhelming was my astonishment that I uttered an involuntary cry, and, running to the skylight, called to Nikola to come on deck. Then, bounding to the bulwarks again, I looked for the boat. But I was too late. Either they had achieved their object, or my prompt action had given them a fright. At any rate, they were gone.

"What do you want?" cried Nikola, who by this time had reached the deck.

"The Chinamen!" I cried. "I saw one of them a moment ago in a boat alongside."

"Where are they now?" he inquired.

"I cannot see them. They have disappeared into the darkness again; but when I called to you they were scarcely twenty yards away. What does their presence here signify, do you think?"

"It signifies that they know that I am on board," answered Nikola, with a queer sort of smile upon his face. "It means also that, although this is the nineteenth century and the law-abiding land of England, if we were to venture a little out of the beaten track ashore to-night, you and I would stand a very fair chance of having our throats cut before morning. It has one other meaning, and that is that you and I must play the old game of the partridge and its nest, and lure them away from this boat while the skipper transfers Don Miguel and his great-granddaughter to the yacht I have in waiting down the river."

"That is all very well," I interrupted, "but I am not at all sure the skipper would be willing. To put it bluntly, he and I have already had a few words together over this matter."

"That will make no difference," Nikola answered. "I assure you you need have no fear that he will play us false: he knows me far too well to attempt that. I will confer with him at once, and while I am doing so you had better get your traps together. We will then go ashore and do our best to draw these rascals off the scent."

So saying, Nikola made his way forward towards the chart room, while I went through the cuddy to my own berth. The steward carried my bags out on to the main deck, and, after I had spoken a word or two with Dona Consuelo, I followed him. Five minutes later Nikola joined me, accompanied by the captain. I had bidden the latter good-bye earlier in the evening, and Nikola was giving him one last word of advice, when I happened to glance towards the alley-way on the port side. Imagine my surprise—nay, I might almost say my consternation—on beholding, standing in the dark by the corner of the main hatch, the same mysterious Chinaman who I felt certain had committed the robbery of the drugs the previous night.

"Look, look," I cried to my companions; "see, there is the man again!"

They wheeled round and looked in the direction to which I pointed. At the same moment the man's right arm went up, and from where I stood I could see something glittering in the palm. An inspiration, how or by what occasioned I shall never be able to understand, induced me to seize Nikola by the arm and to swing him behind me. It was well that I did so, for almost before we could realise what was happening, a knife was thrown, and stood imbedded a good three inches in the bulwark, exactly behind where Nikola had been standing an instant before. Then, springing on to the ladder which leads from the main to the hurricane deck, he raced up it, jumped on to the rail, and dived headlong into the water alongside. By the time we reached the deck whence he had taken his departure, all we could see was a boat pulling swiftly in the direction of the shore.

"That settles it, friend Ingleby," said Nikola.

"We have no alternative now but to make our way ashore and do as I proposed. If you are ready, come along. I think I can safely promise you an adventure."

CHAPTER V. ALLERDEYNE CASTLE

When, nowadays, I look back upon the period I spent in Nikola's company, one significant fact always strikes me, and that is the enormous number of risks we managed to cram into such a comparatively short space of time. During my somewhat chequered career I have perhaps seen as much of what is vaguely termed life as most men: I have lived in countries the very reverse of civilised; I have served aboard ships where there has been a good deal more sandbagging and hazing than would be considered good for the average man's Christian temperament; and as for actual fighting, well, I have seen enough of that to have learnt one lesson—one which will probably cause a smile to rise on the face of the inexperienced—and that is to keep out of it as far as possible, and on all occasions to be afraid of firearms.

I concluded my last chapter with an account of our arrival in Newcastle, and explained how we were preparing to go ashore, when the one-eared Chinaman, who I felt convinced had committed the robbery of the previous night, made his appearance before us and came within an ace of taking Nikola's life. Had it not been for my presence of mind, or instinct, by whichever term you please to call it, I verily believe it would have been the end of all things for the Doctor. As it was, however, the knife missed its mark, and a moment later the man had sprung up the ladder to the hurricane deck and leaped the rail and plunged into the river. Being desirous of preventing the Chinaman from following us and by that means becoming aware that we were leaving for the north in Nikola's yacht, we determined to make our way ashore and permit them to suppose that we were remaining in Newcastle for some length of time. Accordingly we descended into the wherry alongside, and ordered the boatman to pull us to the nearest landing-stage.

"Keep your eyes open and your wits about you," whispered Nikola, when we had left the boat and were making our way up to the street. "They are certain to be on the look-out for us."

As you may be sure, I did not neglect his warning. I had had one exhibition of that diabolical Celestial's skill in knife throwing, and when I reflected that in a big town like Newcastle there were many dark corners and alley-ways, and also that a knife makes but little or no noise when thrown, I was more determined than ever to neglect no opportunity of looking after my own safety. When we reached the street at the rear of the docks Nikola cast about him for a cab, but for some minutes not one was to be seen. At last a small boy obtained one for us, and when the luggage had been placed on the roof we took our seats in it. Nikola gave the driver his instructions, and in a short time we were bowling along in the direction of our hotel. Throughout the drive I could see no signs of the enemy. I was in the act of wondering how such a game as we were then playing could possibly help us if the Celestials had failed to see us come ashore, when Nikola turned to me, and in his usual quiet voice said:

"I wonder if you have noticed that we are being followed?"

I replied that I certainly had not, nor could I see how he could tell such a thing.

"Very easily," he said: "I will prove that what I say is correct. Do you remember the small boy who went in search of a cab?"

I answered that I did, whereupon he bade me examine our reflection as we passed the next shop window. I did so, and could plainly distinguish a small figure seated on the rail at the back. Save this atom, ourselves, and a solitary policeman, the street was deserted.

"I *do* see a small boy," I answered; "but may he not be coming with us to try and obtain the job of carrying our luggage?"

"He is engaged upon another now. When he came up from the river he was on the look-out for us, although, as you may have noticed, he pretended to be asleep in a doorway. He obtained the cab for us, and as you stepped into it he ranged up alongside and handed something to the driver. When we alight he will wait to see that our luggage is carried in, after which he will decamp and carry the information to his employers, who will endeavour to cut our throats as soon as the opportunity occurs."

"You look at the matter in an eminently cheerful light," I said. "For my own part I have no desire to give them the chance just yet. Is there no way in which we can prevent such a possibility occurring?"

"It is for that reason that we are here," Nikola replied. "I can assure you I am no more anxious to die than you are. There would be a good deal of irony in having perfected a scheme for prolonging life, only to meet one's death at the hand of a Chinese ruffian in a civilised English tower."

"Then what is your plan?" I inquired.

"I will tell you. But do not let us speak so loud: little pitchers have long ears. My notion is that we make for the hotel, the name of which I was careful to give the driver in the hearing of the boy. We will engage a couple of rooms there, order breakfast for to-morrow morning, still in the hearing of the boy, and afterwards get out of the way as quietly as possible."

"It sounds feasible enough," I replied, "if only we can do it. But do you think the men will be so easily fooled?"

"Well, that remains to be proved. However, we shall very soon find out."

"A pretty sort of thing you've let yourself in for, Master Ingleby!" I thought to myself as Nikola lapsed into silence once more. "A week ago you were starving in a back street in London, and now it looks very much as if you are going to be murdered in affluence in Newcastle. However, you've let yourself in for it, and have only yourself to blame for the result."

Consoling myself in this philosophic way, I held my peace until the cab drew up before the hostelry to which my companion had alluded. As soon as we were at a standstill, Nikola alighted and went into the hotel to inquire about rooms. As we had agreed, I remained in the cab until he returned.

"It's all right, Ingleby," he cried, as he crossed the pavement again. "They're very full, but we can have the rooms until the day after to-morrow. After that we must look elsewhere. Now let us get the traps inside."

The porter emerged and took our luggage, and we accompanied him into the building. As we did so I saw the ragged urchin who had ridden behind the cab draw near the portico.

The manager received us in the hall. "Numbers 59 and 60," he said to the porter. "Would you care for any supper, gentlemen?" We thanked him, but declined, and then followed the porter upstairs to the rooms in question. Having seen my luggage safely installed and the man on his way downstairs, Nikola showed himself ready for business.

"When you get into these sort of scrapes," he said, "it is just as well to have a good memory. I know these rooms of old, and directly I saw the position we were in I thought they might prove of use to us. I once did the manager a good turn, and when I explain matters to him I fancy he will understand why we have taken up our abode with him only to leave again so suddenly. Have you a sheet of notepaper and an envelope in your bag?"

I produced them for him, whereupon he wrote a note, and having placed a bank-note inside, addressed it to his friend.

"I'll leave it on the chimneypiece, where the chambermaid will be certain to see it," he said. "I have told the manager that we are obliged to leave in this unceremonious fashion in order to rid ourselves of some unpleasant fellow-travellers, who have been following us about with what I can only think must be hostile intent. Until we return I have asked him to take charge of your baggage, so that you need have no fear on that score. I am sorry you should have to lose it, but I can lend you anything you may require until you get possession of it again. Now, if only we can get out of this window and down to the Tyneside once more, without being seen, I think we may safely say we have given Quong Ma the slip for good and all."

So saying he crossed the room and threw open the window.

"We are both active men," Nikola continued, "and should experience small difficulty in dropping on to the roof of the outhouse below; thence we can make our way along the wall to the back. Are you ready?"

"Quite ready," I answered; whereupon he crawled out of the window and, holding on by both hands, lowered himself until his feet were only a yard or so above the roof of the outhouse to which he had referred. Then he let go and dropped. I followed his example, after which we made our way in Indian file along the wall, passed the stables, and dropped without adventure into the dark lane at the rear of the hotel. It was the first time in my life I had left a building of that description in such an unceremonious fashion, yet, strangely enough, I remember, it caused me no surprise. In Nikola's company the most extraordinary performances seemed commonplace, and in the natural order of things.

"From now forward we must proceed with the greatest caution," said my companion, as we regained our feet and paused before making our way down the dark lane towards a small street at the farther end. "They are scarcely likely to watch the back of the hotel, but it will be safer for us to suppose them to be doing so."

Acting up to this decision, we proceeded with as much caution as if every shadow were an enemy and every doorway contained a villainous Celestial. We saw nothing of the men we feared, however, and eventually reached the thoroughfare leading to the docks, without further adventure. But, fortunate as we had been, we were not destined to get away as successfully as we had hoped to do. We were within sight of the river when something, I cannot now remember what, induced me to look back. I did so just in time to catch a glimpse of a figure emerging from the shadow of a tall building. At any other time such a circumstance would have given rise to no suspicion in my mind; but, worked up to such a pitch as I was then, I seemed gifted with an unerring instinct that told me as plainly as any words that the man in question was following us, and that he was the Chinaman we were *so* anxious to avoid. I pointed him out to Nikola, and asked whether he agreed with me as to the man's identity.

"We will soon decide that point," was his reply. "Slacken your pace for a moment, and when I give the word wheel sharply round and walk towards him."

We executed this manoeuvre, and began to walk quickly back in the direction we had come. The mysterious figure was still making his way along the darker side of the street; and our suspicions were soon confirmed, for on seeing us turn he turned also, and a few seconds later disappeared down a side street.

"He is spying on us, sure enough," said Nikola, "and I do not see how we are going to baffle him. Let us hasten on to the river and trust to luck to get on board the yacht without his finding out where we have gone."

Once more we turned ourselves about, and in something less than five minutes had reached the landing-place for which we were steering. Then pulling a whistle from his pocket, Nikola blew three sharp notes upon it. An answer came from the deck of the yacht out in the stream. It had scarcely died away before a boat put off from alongside the craft and came swiftly towards us.

"It is only a question of minutes now," said Nikola, throwing a hasty glance round him. "Time *versus* the Chinaman, and if I am not mistaken "—here the boat drew up at the steps—"time has the best of it. Come along, my friend; let us get on board."

I followed him down the steps and took my place in the dinghy. The men pulling bent to their oars, and we shot out into the stream.

"Look," said Nikola, pointing to the place we had just left: "I thought our friend would not be very far behind us."

I followed with my eyes the direction in which he pointed, and, sure enough, I could just distinguish a dark figure standing upon the steps.

"They would like to catch me if they could," observed the Doctor, with a shrug of his shoulders and one of his peculiar laughs. "If they have tried once they have done so a hundred times. I will do them the credit of saying that their plans have been admirably laid, but Fate has stood by me, and on each occasion they have miscarried. They tried it first at Ya-Chow-Fu, then at I-chang, afterwards in Shanghai, Rangoon, Bombay, London, Paris, and St. Petersburg, and I can't tell you how many other places; but as you see, they have not succeeded so far."

"But why should they do it?" I asked. "What is the reason of it all?"

"That is too long a story for me to tell you now," he replied, as the boat drew up at the accommodation-ladder. "You shall hear it another day. Our object now must be to get away from Newcastle without further loss of time."

I followed him along the deck to where a short stout man stood waiting to receive *us*.

"Are you ready, Stevens?" asked Nikola.

"All ready, sir," the other replied, with the brevity of a man who is not accustomed to waste his words.

"In that case let us start as quickly as possible."

"At once," the man replied, and immediately went forward; while Nikola conducted me down a prettily arranged and constructed companion-ladder to the saloon below. As we reached it I heard the tinkle of the telegraph from the bridge to the engine room, and almost simultaneously the screw began to revolve and we were under way. After the darkness outside, the brilliant light of the saloon in which we now stood was so dazzling that I failed to notice the fact that a bedplace had been made up behind the butt of the mizzen mast. Upon this lay the old Don, and seated by his side, and holding his hand, was the Dona Consuelo.

"My dear young lady," said Nikola in his kindest manner, as he advanced towards her, "I fear you must be worn out. However, we are under way again now, and I have instructed my servant to prepare a cabin for you, in which I trust you will be fairly comfortable."

Dona Consuelo had risen, and was standing looking into his face as if she were frightened of something he was about to say.

"I am not at all tired," she said, "and if you don't mind, I would far rather remain here with my great-grandfather."

"As you wish," answered Nikola abstractedly. Then, stooping, he raised the old man's left hand and felt his pulse. The long, thin fingers of the Doctor, indicative of his extraordinary skill as a surgeon, seemed to twine round the other's emaciated wrist, while his face wore a look I had never seen upon it before—it was that of the born enthusiast, the man who loves his profession more than aught else in the world. While, however, I was observing Nikola, you must not suppose I was regardless of the Dona Consuelo. To a student of character, the expression upon her face could scarcely have been anything but interesting. While Nikola was conducting his examination, she watched him as if she dreaded what he might do next. Fear there was in abundance, but of admiration for the man I could discover no trace. The examination concluded, Nikola addressed two or three pertinent questions to her concerning her great-grandfather's health during the voyage, which she answered with corresponding clearness and conciseness. The old man himself, however, though conscious, did not utter a word, but lay staring up at the skylight above his head, just as I had seen him do on board the *Dotta Mercedes*.

Fully five hours must have elapsed before we reached our destination; indeed, day had broken, and the sun was in the act of rising, when a gentle tapping upon the skylight overhead warned Nikola that our voyage was nearly at an end. Leaving the old man in his great-granddaughter's care, Nikola signed to me to follow him to the deck.

"It may interest you to see your future home," he said, as we stepped out of the companion into the cool morning air, and looked out over the sea, which the rim of the newly risen sun was burnishing until it shone like polished silver. At the moment the yacht was entering a small bay, surrounded by giant cliffs, against which the great rollers of the North Sea broke continuously. The bay itself was in deep shadow, and was as dreary a place as any I have seen. I looked about me for a dwelling of any sort, but not a sign of such a thing could I discover: only a long stretch of frowning cliff and desolate, wind-swept tableland.

"At first glance it does not look inviting," said Nikola, with a smile upon his face, as he noticed the expression upon mine. "I confess I have seen a more hospitable coast-line, but never one better fitted for the work we have in hand."

"But I do not see the castle," I replied. "I have looked in every direction, but can discover no trace of it."

"One of its charms," he continued triumphantly. "You cannot see it because at present it is hidden by yonder headland. When we are safely in the bay, however, you will have a good view of it. It is a fine old building, and in bygone days must have been a place of considerable importance. Ships innumerable have gone to pieces in sight of its turrets; while deep down in its own foundations I am told there are dungeons enough to imprison half the county. See, we are opening up the bay now, and in five minutes shall be at anchor. I wonder what result we shall have achieved when we next steam between these heads."

While he was speaking we had passed from the open sea into the still water of the bay, and the yacht was slowing down perceptibly. Gradually the picture unfolded itself, until, standing out in bold relief upon the cliffs like some grim sentinel of the past, the castle which, for some time to come at least, was destined to be my home came into view. Who its architect had been I was never able to discover, but he must have been impregnated with the desolation and solemn grandeur of the coast, and in his building have tried to equal it. As Nikola had said, a place better fitted for the work we had come to do could not have been discovered in the length and breadth of England. The nearest village was upwards of twelve miles distant; farms or dwelling-houses there were none within view of its towers. Tourists seldom ventured near it, for the reason that it was not only a place difficult of approach, but, what was perhaps of more importance, because there was nothing of interest to be seen when you reached it. As I gazed at it, I thought of the girl in the saloon below, and wondered what her feelings would be, and what her life would be like, in such a dismal place. I glanced at Nikola, who was gazing up at the grim walls with such rapt attention that it was easily seen his thoughts were far away. Then the telegraph sounded, and the screw ceased to revolve, The spell was broken, and we were recalled to the realities of the moment.

"I was miles away," said Nikola, looking round at me.

"I could see you were," I answered.

"You would be very surprised if you knew of what I was thinking," he continued. "I was recalling a place not unlike this, but ten thousand miles or more away. It is a monastery, similarly situated, on the top of enormous cliffs. It was there I obtained the secret which is the backbone of the discovery we are about to test. I have been in some queer places in my time, but never such a one as that. But we haven't time to talk of that now. What we have to do is to get the old man ashore and up to yonder building. If anything were to happen to him now, I think it would break my heart."

"And his great-granddaughter's also," I put in; "for you must admit she is devoted to him."

He threw a quick glance at me, as if he were trying to discern how far I was interested in the beautiful girl in the saloon below. Whatever conclusion he may have come to, however, he said nothing to me upon the subject. Having ordered the captain to see the boat—which had been specially prepared for the work of carrying the old gentleman ashore—brought alongside, he made his way to the saloon, and I accompanied him.

"We have reached our destination, Dona Consuelo," he said, as he approached the bed, beside which she was sitting.

As he spoke, there leapt into her eyes the same look of terror I had noticed before. It reminded me more than anything else of the expression one sees in the eyes of a rabbit when the snare has closed upon it. As I noticed it, for the first time since I had known him, a feeling of hatred for Nikola came over me. It was not until we were in the boat and were making our way ashore that I found an opportunity of speaking to her without Nikola overhearing us.

"Courage, my dear young lady, courage!" I said. "Believe me, there is nothing to fear. I will pledge my life for your safety."

She gave me a look of gratitude, and stooped as if to arrange the heavy travelling-rug covering her aged relative. In reality I believe it was to hide the tears with which her eyes were filled. From that moment there existed an indefinable, real bond between us; and though I did not realise it at the moment, the first mark had been made upon the chain with which Nikola imagined he had bound me to him.

On reaching that side of the bay on which there was a short strip of beach, the boat was grounded. The four sailors immediately took up the litter upon which the old man lay, and carried it ashore. The path up to the castle was a steep and narrow one, and the work of conveying him to the top was by no means easy. Eventually, however, it was accomplished, and we stood before the entrance to the castle. Moat there was none, but in place of it, and spanned by the drawbridge—a ponderous affair, something like fifty feet long by ten wide—was an enormous chasm going sheer down in one drop fully two hundred feet. At the bottom water could be seen; and at night, when the tide came in, the gurgling and moaning that rose from it was sufficient to appal the stoutest heart.

"Welcome to Allerdeyne Castle!" said Nikola, as we crossed the bridge and entered the archway of the ancient keep. Then, bending over the old man on the litter, he added: "When you cross this threshold again, my old friend, I hope that you will be fully restored to health and strength—a young man again in every sense of the word. Dona Consuelo, I am all anxiety to hear your opinion of the apartments I have caused to be prepared for you."

Moving in procession as before, we crossed the great courtyard, which echoed to the sound of our footsteps, and, reaching a door on the farther side, entered and found ourselves standing in a well-proportioned hall, from which a staircase of solid stone, up which a dozen soldiers might have marched abreast, led to the floors above. With Nikola still in advance, we made the ascent, turned to the right hand, and proceeded along a corridor, upwards of fifty yards in length, out of which opened a number of lofty rooms. Before the door of one of these Nikola paused.

"This is the apartment I have set aside for your own particular use, my dear young lady," he said; and with that he threw open the door, and showed us a large room, carpeted, curtained, and furnished in a fashion I was far from expecting to find in so sombre a building.

"Should there be anything wanting," he said, "you will honour me by mentioning it, when I will do all that lies in my power to supply it."

Her face was very pale, and her lips trembled a little as she faltered a question as to where her great-grandfather was to be domiciled.

"I have come to the conclusion that, for the future, it would be better," said Nikola, speaking very slowly and distinctly, as if in anticipation of future trouble, "that you should entrust him to my care. Ingleby and I, between us, will make ourselves responsible for his safety, and you may rest assured we will see that no harm comes to him. You must endeavour to amuse yourself as best you can, consoling yourself with the knowledge that we are doing all that science can do for him."

As he said this he smiled a little sarcastically, as if her reading of the word science would be likely to differ considerably from his.

"But surely you do not mean that I am to give him up to you entirely?" she cried, this time in real terror. "You cannot be so cruel as to mean that. Oh, Dr. Nikola, I implore you not to take him altogether from me. I cannot bear it."

"My dear young lady," said Nikola, a little more sternly than he had yet spoken, "in this matter you must be guided by me. I can brook no interference of any description. Surely you should know me well enough by this time to be aware of that."

"But he is all I have to live for—all I have to love," the girl faltered. "Can you not make allowance for that?"

Her voice was piteous in its pleading, and when I heard Nikola's chilling tones as he answered her, I could have found it in my heart to strike him. To have interfered at all, however, would have done no sort of good; so, hard as it seemed, I was perforce compelled to hold my tongue.

"If you love your great-grandfather," he said, "you will offer no opposition to my scheme. Have I not already assured you that I will return him to you a different man? But we are wasting time, and these stone corridors are too cold and draughty for him. If you will be guided by me, you will rest a little after your exertions. There is an old woman below who shall come to you, and do her best to make herself useful to you." Seeing that to protest further would be useless, the girl turned and went into the room, trying to stifle the sobs that would not be kept back. The sight was one which would have grieved a harder heart than mine, and it hurt me the more because I knew that I was powerless to help her.

All this time the four sailors, who had carried the litter up from the beach, had been silent spectators of the scene. Now they took up their burden once more and followed Nikola, along the corridor, up some more steps, down still another passage, until I lost all count of the way that we had come. The greater portion of the castle had been allowed to fall into disrepair. Heavy masses of cobwebs stretched from wall to wall, a large proportion of the doors were worm-eaten, and in some instances had even fallen in altogether, revealing desolate apartments, in which the wind from the sea whistled, and the noise of the waves echoed with blood-curdling effect. Reaching the end of the second corridor, Nikola paused before a heavy curtain which was drawn closely from wall to wall, and ordered the men to set down their burden. They obeyed; and, on being told to do so, took their departure with as much speed as they could put into the operation. If I know anything of the human face, they were not a little relieved at receiving permission to clear out of a place that had every right to be considered the abode of a certain Old Gentleman whom it scarcely becomes me to mention.

When the sound of their footsteps had died away, Nikola drew back the curtain and displayed a plain but very strong wooden door. From the fact that the workmanship was almost new I surmised that my host had placed it there himself, but for what purpose I could only conjecture. Taking a key from his pocket, he slipped it into the patent lock, turned the handle, and the door swung open.

"Take up your end of the litter," he said, "and help me to carry it inside."

I did as I was ordered; and, bearing the old man between us, we passed into that portion of the castle which, as I soon discovered, he had fitted up in readiness for the great experiment.

" Trying to stifle the sobs that would not keep back."

Having passed the door, we found ourselves in a comparatively lofty room, or perhaps I had better say hall, the walls of which were covered almost entirely with anatomical specimens. From what I could see of them I should say that many of them were quite unique, while all were extremely valuable. Where and by what means he had collected them I was never able to discover, although Nikola, on one or two occasions, threw out hints. There they were, however, and I promised myself that during my stay in the place I would use them for perfecting my own knowledge on the subject.

At the end of this hall, and looking over the sea, was a large window, while in either wall were several doors, all of which, like that in the corridor, were heavily curtained. The carpet was of cork and quite noiseless; the lights were electric, the batteries and dynamos being in a room below. The heating arrangements were excellent, while the ventilation was of the most modern and improved description. I noticed that Nikola smiled a little contemptuously at my astonishment.

"You were unprepared for this surprise," he said. "Well, let me give you a little piece of advice, and that is, never be astonished at anything you may see or hear while you are with me. The commonplace and I, I can assure you once and for all, do not live together. I have homes in all parts of the world; I am in England to-day, engaged upon one piece of work, and in six months' time I may be in India, Japan, Peru, Kamtschatka, or if you like it better, shall we say playing tricks with niggers in Cape Coast Castle? But see, we are keeping our old friend waiting. I will find out if all the preparations I have ordered are complete; if so, we will convey him at once to the chamber set apart for him."

With that he touched a bell, and almost before he had removed his finger from the button, a curtain at the farther end was drawn aside, and the same Chinese servant—the deaf-and-dumb individual, I mean, who had brought the letter to me at my lodgings in London the previous week—entered the room. Seeing his master, he bent himself nearly double, and when he had resumed his upright posture as curious a conversation commenced as ever I have known.

I use the word "conversation" for the simple reason that I do not know how else to describe it. As a matter of fact it was not a conversation at all, for the reason that not a word was spoken on either side; their lips moved, but not a sound came from them. And yet they seemed quite able to understand one another. If, however, it was a strange performance, it had at least the merit of being an extremely successful one.

"He tells me that everything is prepared," Nikola remarked, as the man crossed the room and drew back another curtain from a doorway on our left. "This is the room; but before we carry him into it I think we had better have a little light upon the subject."

To press the electric switch was the work of a moment, and as soon as this had been done we once more took up our burden and carried it into the inner room. Prepared as I had been by the outer hall for something extraordinary, I was perhaps not so much surprised at the apartment in which I now found myself as I should otherwise have been. And yet it was sufficiently remarkable to fill any one with wonder.

It was upwards of twenty feet in length by possibly eighteen in width. The walls and the ceilings were as black as charcoal, and, when the electric light was extinguished, not a ray of anything would be visible. In the centre was a strange contrivance which I could see was intended to serve as a bed, and for some other purpose, which at the moment was not quite apparent to me. In the farther corners were a couple of queer-looking pieces of machinery, one of which reminded me somewhat of an unusually large electric battery; the other I could not understand at all. A machine twice the size of those usually employed for manufacturing ozone stood opposite the door; thermometers of every sort and description were arranged at intervals along the walls; while on one side was an ingenious apparatus for heating the room, and on the other a similar one for cooling it. At the head and foot of the bed were two brass pillars, the construction and arrangements of which reminded me of electric terminals on an exaggerated scale.

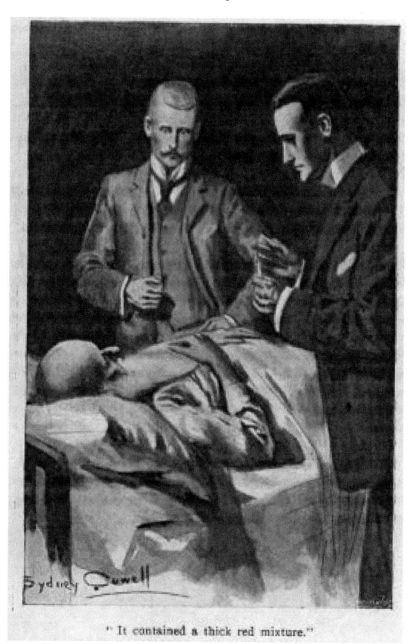

"It contained a thick red mixture."

We placed the old gentleman on the bed. The litter was thereupon removed by the servant, and Nikola and I stood facing each other across the form of the man who was to prove, or disprove, the feasibility of the discovery my extraordinary employer claimed to have made.

"For twenty-four hours," said Nikola, "he must have absolute peace and quiet. Nothing must disturb him. Nor must he taste food."

"But is he capable, do you think," I asked, "of going without nourishment for so long a time?"

"Perfectly! On the draught I am about to administer to him, he could do without it, were such a thing necessary, for a much longer period. Indeed, it would not hurt him if he were to eat nothing for a month."

He left the room for a moment, and when he returned he carried in his hand a tiny phial of the same description, though much smaller, as those which had been stolen from me on board the steamer. It contained a thick, red mixture, which, when he removed the stopper, threw off a highly pungent odour. He opened the mouth of the patient and poured upwards of a teaspoonful into it. As before, I expected to see some immediate result, but my curiosity was not gratified. Deftly arranging the bed-coverings, Nikola inspected the thermometers, tested the hot and cold air apparatus, and then turned to me.

"He will require little or no supervision for some hours to come," he said, "so we may safely leave him. To while away the time, if you care about it, I will show you something of my abode. I think I can promise you both instruction and amusement."

CHAPTER VI. LIFE IN THE CASTLE

LEAVING the room in which we had placed Don Miguel de Moreno, as described in the previous chapter, we returned to the hall, the same in which was contained the magnificent collection of anatomical specimens already mentioned. Tired as I was,—for it must be remembered that I had had but little sleep during the first night I had spent on board the *Dona Mercedes,* and none at all on that through which we had just passed, while I had had a great deal of excitement, and my fair share of hard work,—I would not have lost the opportunity of exploring Nikola's quarters in this grim old castle for any consideration whatsoever. Nikola himself, though one would scarcely have thought it from his appearance, must have possessed a constitution of iron, for he seemed as fresh as when I had first seen him at Kelleran's house in London. There was a vitality about him, a briskness, and, if I may so express it, an enjoyment of labour for its own sake, that I do not remember ever to have found in another man. As I was soon to discover, my description of him was not very wide of the mark. He would do the work of half a dozen men, and at the end be ready, and not only ready but eager, for more. In addition to this, I noticed another peculiarity about him. Unlike most people who are fond of work, he possessed an infinite fund of patience; could wait for an issue, whatever it might be, to develop itself naturally, and, unlike so many experimentalists, betrayed no desire to hurry it by the employment of extraneous means. In thus putting forward my reading of the most complex character that has ever come under my notice, I do so with an absolute freedom from bias. Indeed, I might almost say, that I do so in a great measure against my own inclinations, as will be apparent to you when you have finished my story.

"As I informed you in London," said this strange individual, after he had closed the door of the patient's room behind him, had drawn the heavy curtain, and switched off the electric light, "I purchased this famous castle expressly for the experiment we are about to try. The owner, so my business people informed me, was amazed that I should want it at all; but then, you see, he did not understand its value. If I had searched the world, I could not have discovered a better. While we are near enough to civilisation to be able to obtain anything we may require in the way of drugs or incidental apparatus, we have no prying neighbours; such household stores as we require the yacht brings us direct from Newcastle; an old man and woman, who take care of the place when I am absent, have their quarters in the keep; my Chinese servant cooks for me personally, and attends to the wants, which are not many, of the other people under my care."

"Other people under your care?" I echoed. "I had no idea there was any one in the house save yourself and your servants."

"It is scarcely likely you would have any idea of it," he observed, "seeing that no one knows of it save Ah-Win, who, for reasons you have seen, is unable to talk about them, and myself, who would be even less likely to do so. Would you care to see them?"

I replied that I would very much like to do so, and he was about to lead me across the hall towards the door, through which the Chinese servant had entered some little time before, when a curious circumstance happened. With a bound that was not unlike the spring of a tiger, an enormous cat, black as the Pit of Tophet, jumped from the room, and, approaching his master, rubbed himself backwards and forwards against his legs. Seeing my astonishment, Nikola condescended to explain.

"You are going to say, I can tell, that you have never seen such a cat as Apollyon. I don't suppose you have. If he could talk, he would be able to tell some strange stories; would you not, old man? He has been my almost constant companion for many years, and more than once he has been the means of saving my life."

Replacing Apollyon, whom he had picked up, on the floor, he conducted me towards the entrance of another corridor which led in the direction of the keep. Half-way down it was a rough iron gate, which was securely padlocked.

Nikola undid it, and when we were on the other side carefully relocked it after him.

"Though you might not think so," he said, "these precautions are necessary. Some of my patients are extremely valuable, and I have not the least desire that they should escape from my keeping and fall over the battlements into the sea below. Follow me."

I accompanied him towards yet another door, which he also unlocked. The scene which met my gaze when he threw it open, to employ a hackneyed phrase, beggars description. The room was about the same size as that occupied by the Dona Consuelo, but it was not its proportions that amazed me, but its occupants. Accustomed as I had necessarily been, by virtue of my profession, to what are commonly called horrors, I found that I was not proof against what I had before me now. It was sufficient to make my blood run cold. Anything more gruesome could scarcely have been discovered or even imagined. Try to picture for yourself the inmates of a dozen freak museums, and the worst of the monstrosities of which you have ever read or heard, and you will only have some dim notion of the folk whom Nikola so ironically called his patients. Some were like men, but not men as we know them; some were like monkeys, but of a kind I had never seen before, and which I sincerely hope I may never see again; there were things, dull, flabby, faceless things—but there, I can go no farther. To attempt to describe them to you in detail is a work of which my pen is quite incapable.

"A happy family," said Nikola, advancing into the room, "and without exception devoted to their nurse, Ah-Win, yonder, who, as you are aware, in a measure shares their afflictions with them. Some day, if you care about it, I should be only too pleased to give you a lecture, with demonstrations, such as you would get in no medical school in the world."

Though I have attempted to set down his offer word for word, I have but the vaguest recollection of it; for, long before he had finished speaking, I had staggered, sick and faint with horror, into the corridor outside. Not for the wealth of England would I have remained there a minute longer. To see those loathsome creatures fawning round Nikola, clutching at his legs and stroking his clothes, was too much for me, and I verily believe an hour in that room would have had the effect of making me an idiot like themselves. A few moments later Nikola joined me in the passage.

"You are very easily affected, my dear Ingleby," he said, with one of his peculiar smiles. "I should have thought your hospital experience would have endowed you with stronger nerves. My poor people in yonder—"

"Don't, don't," I cried, holding up my hand in entreaty. "Don't speak to me of them. Don't let me think of them. If I do, I believe I shall go mad. My God! are you human, that you can live with such things about you?"

"I believe I am," he answered with the utmost coolness. "But why make such a fuss? Do like I do, and regard them from a scientific standpoint only. The poor things have come into this world handicapped by misfortune; I endeavour as far as possible to ameliorate their conditions, and in return they enable me to perfect my knowledge of the human frame as no other living man can ever hope to do. Of course, I know there are people who look askance at me for keeping them; but that does not trouble me. At one time they lived with me in Port Said, which, when you come to think of it, is a fit and proper place for such a hospital. Circumstances, however, combined to induce me to leave. Eventually we came here. Some time, if you care to hear it, I will tell you the story of their voyage home. It would interest you."

I protested, however, that I desired to hear no more about them; I had both seen and heard too much already. That being so, Nikola led me along the passage and through the iron gate, which he locked behind him as before, and so conducted me to the hall whence we had first set out. Once there, he went to a corner cabinet, and from it produced a decanter. Pouring me out a stiff glass of brandy, he bade me drink it.

"You look as if you want it," he said. And Heaven knows he was right.

"And now," he said, when I had finished it, "if you will take my advice, you will lie down for an hour or two. For the convenience of our work, I have arranged that you shall occupy a room near me. This is it. Should I want you, I will ring a bell."

The room to which he alluded adjoined his own, and was situated at the far end of the hall, the door, like those of the others I have described, being concealed behind a curtain. Never was permission to retire more willingly accepted, and within five minutes of leaving him I was in bed and asleep.

It must have been between ten and eleven o'clock in the forenoon when I retired; and the afternoon was well advanced before I woke again. Heavily as I slept, however, it had not been restful slumber. All things considered, I had much better have been waking.

Over and over again I saw the Dona Consuelo standing before me, just as she had done before Nikola that day; there was this difference, however—instead of asking to be allowed to remain with her great-grandfather, her prayer was that I should save both him and her from Nikola. While she pleaded to me, the faces of the terrible creatures I had seen in that room down the passage peered at us from all sorts of hiding-places. It was night, an hour or so before dawn. I had acceded to the Dona's request, and was flying from the castle, carrying her in my arms.

At last, after I appeared to have been running for an eternity, we reached the shore, where I hoped to find a boat awaiting us. But not a sign of one was to be seen. While I waited day broke, and I placed my burden on the sand, only to spring back from it with a cry of horror. It was not the Dona Consuelo I had been carrying, but one of those loathsome creatures I had seen in that terrible room. A fit of rage came over me, and I was about to wreak my vengeance on the unhappy idiot, when I woke. I looked about me at the somewhat sparsely furnished room, and some seconds elapsed before I realised where I was. Then the memory of our arrival at the castle, and of all that had happened since, returned to me. I shuddered, and had it not been for that poor girl, so lonely and friendless, I could have found it in my heart to wish myself back in London once more. Having dressed myself, I went out into the hall. Nikola was not there. I waited for some time, but as he did not put in an appearance I left the room and made my way down the corridor in the direction of the Dona Consuelo's sitting-room. Not able to get any answer when I knocked, I continued my walk, ascended another flight of stairs, and eventually found myself upon the battlements. A better place for observing the construction of the castle, and of obtaining a view of the surrounding country, could not have been desired. On one side I could look away across the moorland towards a distant range of hills, and on the other along the cliffs and across the wide expanse of sea. In the tiny bay to my right the yacht which had brought us from Newcastle lay at anchor; and had it not been for that and a column of grey smoke rising from a chimney, I might have believed myself to be living in a world of my own. For some time I stood watching the panorama spread out before me. I was still looking at it when a soft footfall sounded on the stones behind me. I turned to find Dona Consuelo approaching me. She was dressed entirely in black, and wore a lace mantilla over her shoulders.

"Thank Heaven, I have found you, Dr. Ingleby," she cried, as she hastened towards me. "I had begun to think myself deserted by everybody."

"Why should you do that?" I asked. "You know that could never be."

"I am certain of nothing now," she answered. "You cannot imagine what I have been through to-day."

"I am indeed sorry to hear you have been unhappy," I continued. "Is there any way in which I can be of service to you?"

"There are many ways, but I fear you would not employ them," she replied. "I am hungering to be with my great-grandfather again. Can you tell me why Dr. Nikola takes him away from me?"

"I fancied that he had told you," I answered; "but if it be any consolation to you, let me give you my assurance that he is tenderly cared for. His comfort is secured in every way; and from what Dr. Nikola has said to me, and from what I have seen myself, I feel convinced he will be able to do what he has promised and make your great-grandfather a hale and hearty man once more."

"It is all very well for him to say that," she said, "but why am I not permitted to be with him? If he needs nursing, who would be likely to wait upon him so devotedly as the woman who loves him? Surely Dr. Nikola cannot imagine his secret would be unsafe with me if he reveals it to you, a rival in his own profession?"

"It is not that at all," I answered. "I do not fancy Nikola has given a moment's consideration to the safety of his secret." Then, seeing the loophole of escape she presented to me, I added: "From what you know of him, I should have thought you would have understood that he has no great liking for your sex. To put it bluntly, Nikola is a woman-hater of the most determined order, and I fancy he would find it impossible to carry out his plans if you were in attendance upon the Don."

"Ah well! I suppose I must be content with your assurance," she said with a sigh.

"For the present, I am very much afraid so," I replied.

At this moment the old woman whom Nikola had appointed to wait upon us made her appearance, and informed the Dona that her dinner awaited her. About my own meals she knew nothing, so I concluded from this that I was to take them with Nikola in our own portion of the castle. Such proved to be the case; for when we reached the Dona Consuelo's apartments on the floor below, we met Nikola awaiting us in the corridor.

"I have been looking for you, Ingleby," he said, with a note of command in his voice. "You are quite ready for dinner, I have no doubt; and if you will accompany me, I think we shall find it waiting for us."

As may be supposed, I would rather have partaken of it with Dona Consuelo; but as it was not to be, I bade her good morning, and was about to follow Nikola along the corridor, when he stopped, and, turning to the girl, said:

"I can see from your face that you have been worrying about your grandfather. I assure you, you have not the least cause to do so; and I think Ingleby here, if he has not done so already, will bear me out in what I say. The old gentleman is doing excellently, and almost before you know he has been taken away from you, you will have him back again."

"I thank you for your news," she replied; but there was very little friendliness in her voice. "I would rather, however, see him and convince myself of the fact." Then, bowing to us, she retired into her own apartments, while we made our way to the hall in search of our meal.

"To-morrow morning," said Nikola, as we drew our chairs up to the table, "we must commence work in earnest. After that for some weeks to come I am afraid you will see but little of your fair friend down yonder. You seem to be on excellent terms with one another."

As he said this he shot a keen glance at me, as though he were desirous of discovering what was passing in my mind. I was quite prepared for him, however, and answered in such an unconcerned way that I nattered(?) myself, should he have got it into his head that there was anything more than mere friendship in our intimacy, he would be immediately disabused of the notion.

As he had predicted, the following morning saw the commencement of that gigantic struggle with the forces of Nature, upon the result of which Nikola had pinned so much faith and which was destined, so he affirmed, to revolutionise the world. The most exhaustive preparations had been made, the duration of our watches in the sick-room were duly apportioned, and a minute outline of the treatment proposed was propounded to me.

On entering the dark room in which the old Don lay, I discovered that the two bronze pedestals, the use of which had puzzled me so much on my first visit, had been moved near the bed, one been placed at its head and the other at its foot. These, as Nikola pointed out to me, were the terminals of an electric conductor for producing a constant current, which was to play without intermission a few feet above the patient's head. A peculiar and penetrating smell filled the room, which I had no difficulty in recognising as ozone, though Nikola's reason for using it in such a case was not at first apparent to me. The old Don himself lay just as we had left him the previous morning. His hands were by his sides; his eyes, as usual, were open, but saw nothing. It was not until I examined him closely that a slight respiratory movement was observable.

"When I am not here," said Nikola, "it must be your business to see that this electric current is kept continually playing above him. It must not be permitted for an instant to abate one unit of its strength." Then, pointing to an instrument fixed at the further wall, he continued: "Here is a volt meter, with the maximum and minimum points plainly marked upon it Your record must also include temperature, which you will take on these dry and wet thermometers once every quarter of an hour. The currents of hot and cold air you can regulate by means of these handles. The temperature of the patient himself must be noted once in every hour, and should on no account be permitted to get higher or lower than it is at the present moment."

Taking a clinical thermometer from his pocket, he applied it, and, when he had noted the result, handed it to me.

"If it rises two points above that before the same hour three days hence, he will die—no skill can save him. If it drops, well, in eighty per cent, of cases, the result will be the same."

"And suppose I detect a tendency to rise?"

"In that case you must communicate instantly with me. Here is an electric button which will put you in touch with my room. I hope, however, that you will have no necessity to use it." Then, placing his hand upon my shoulder, he looked me full in the face. "Ingleby," he said, "you see how much trust I am placing in you. I tell you frankly, you have a great responsibility upon your shoulders. I am not going to beat about the bush with you. In this case there is no such thing as certainty. I have made the attempt three times before, and on each occasion my man has died simply through a moment's inattention on the part of my assistant. If the love of our science and a proper appreciation of the compliment I have paid you in asking you to share with me the honour of this great discovery do not weigh with you, think of the girl with whom you talked upon the battlements yesterday. You tried to make me believe that she was nothing to you. Some day, however, she may be. Remember what her grandfather's death would mean to her."

"You need have no fear," I replied. "I assure you, you can trust me implicitly."

"I do trust you," he answered. "Now let us get to work."

So saying, he crossed the room and opened a square box, heavily clamped with iron, from which he took two china pots of ointment. Then, disrobing the old man, we anointed him with the most scrupulous care from head to foot. This we did three times, after which the second curious apparatus I had seen standing in the corner was wheeled up to the bedside. That it was an electrical instrument of some sort was plain, but what its specific use was I could not even conjecture. Nikola, however, very soon enlightened me upon the matter. Taking a number of large velvet pads, each of which was moulded to fit a definite portion of the human body, he placed them in position, attached the wires that connected them with the machine, and when all was ready turned on the current. At first no effect was observable. In about a minute and a half, however, if my memory serves me, the usual deathly pallor of the skin gave place to a faint blush, which presently increased until the skin exhibited a healthy glow; little by little the temporal veins, until then so prominent, gradually disappeared. In half an hour, during which the current had been slowly and very gradually increased, another dressing of both ointments was applied.

"Take this glass and examine his skin," said Nikola, whose eyes were gleaming with excitement, as he handed me a powerful magnifying glass. When I bent over the patient and did as he directed, it was indeed a wonderful thing that I beheld. An hour before the skin had been soft and hung in loose folds upon the bones, while the pressure of a finger upon it would not leave it for upwards of a minute. Now it had in a measure regained its youthful elasticity, and upon my softly pinching it between my fingers I found that it recovered its colour almost immediately.

"It is wonderful," I whispered. "Had I not seen it myself, I would never have believed it."

When it had been applied for an hour, the electric current was turned off and the pads removed.

"Now watch what happens very closely," said Nikola, "for, I assure you, the effect is curious."

Scarcely able to breathe by reason of my excitement, I watched, and as I did so I saw the flush of apparent health gradually decrease, the skin become white and loose once more, while the superficial veins rose into prominence upon the temples. I glanced at Nikola, thinking that some mistake must have occurred and that he would show signs of disappointment. This, however, he did not do.

"You surely did not imagine," he said, when I had questioned him upon the subject, "that the effect I produced would be permanent on the first application? No! we may hope to achieve a more lasting result in a fortnight's time, but not till then.

"Meanwhile, the effect must be produced in the same fashion every six hours, both day and night. Now give me those rugs; we must cover him carefully. In his present state the least draught would be fatal. Record the state of the volt meter, read your thermometers, and see that your ventilating apparatus is working properly. As I said just now, should you need me, remember the bell. One ring, when you have recorded your results, will inform me that all is progressing satisfactorily, while three will immediately bring me to your assistance. Do you understand?"

When I had assured him that I did, he left me. I accordingly switched off three of the electric lights, and sat myself down in a chair in semi-darkness, the centre of light being the patient on the bed. There was no fear of my feeling dull, for I had a great deal to think about. Taken altogether, the situation in which I found myself was as extraordinary as the most inveterate seeker after excitement could desire. Not a sound was to be heard. The stillness was that of the tomb, and yet I smiled to myself as I thought that, if Nikola's experiment achieved the result he expected of it, the simile was not an appropriate one, for it was not the silence of the tomb but of perpetual life itself. I looked at the figure on the bed before me, and tried to picture what the mystery he was unravelling would mean to mankind. It was a solemn thought. Should the experiment prove successful, how would it affect the world? Would it prove a blessing or a curse? But the thoughts it conjured up were too vast, the issues too great, and to attempt to solve them was only to lose oneself in the fields of wildest conjecture.

For four hours I remained on duty, noting all that occurred; reading my thermometers, regulating the hot and cold air apparatus, and at intervals signalling to Nikola that everything was progressing satisfactorily. When he relieved me, I retired to rest and slept like a top, too tired even to dream.

Of what happened during the fortnight following I have little to tell. Nikola and I watched by the bedside in turn, took our exercise upon the battlements, ate and slept with the regularity of automata. The life on one side was monotonous in the extreme; on the other it was filled with an unholy excitement that was the greater inasmuch as it had to be so carefully suppressed. To say that I was deeply interested in the work upon which I was engaged would be a by no means strong enough expression. The fire of enthusiasm, to which I have before alluded, was raging once more in my heart, and yet there had been little enough so far in the experiment to excite it. With that regularity which characterised the whole of our operations, we carried on the work I have described. Every sixth hour saw the skin tighten and become elastic, the hue of the flesh change from white to pink, the veins recede, and the hollows fill, only to return to their original state as soon as the electric current was withdrawn. Towards the end of the fortnight, however, there were not wanting signs to show that the effect was gradually becoming more lasting. In place of doing so at once, the change to the original condition did not occur until some eight or ten minutes after the pads had been removed. And here I must remark that there was one other point in the case which struck me as peculiar. When I had first seen the old man, his finger-nails were of that pale yellow tint so often observable in the very old, now they were a delicate shade of pink; while his hair was, I felt convinced, a darker shade than it had been before. As Nikola was careful to point out, we had arrived at the most critical stage of the experiment. A mistake at this juncture, would not only undo all the work we had accomplished, but, what was more serious still, might very possibly cost us the life of the patient himself.

The night I am about to describe was at the end of the fourteenth day after our arrival at the castle. Nikola had been on watch from four o'clock in the afternoon until eight, when I relieved him.

"Do not let your eyes wander from him for a minute," he said, as I took my place beside the bed. "From certain symptoms I have noticed during the last few hours, I am convinced the crisis is close at hand. Should a rise in the temperature occur, summon me instantly. I shall be in the laboratory ready at a moment's notice to prepare the elixir upon which the success we hope to achieve depends."

"But you are worn out," I said, as I noticed the haggard expression upon his face. "Why don't you take some rest?"

"Rest!" he cried scornfully. "Is it likely that I could rest with such a discovery just coming within my grasp? No; you need not fear for me; I shall not break down. I have a constitution of iron."

Having once more warned me to advise him of any change that might occur, he left me; and when I had examined my instruments, attended to the electrical apparatus, and taken the patient's temperature, I sat down to the vigil to which I had by this time become accustomed. Hour by hour I followed the customary routine. My watch was early at an end. In twenty minutes it would be time for Nikola to relieve me. Leaning over the old man, I convinced myself that no change had taken place in his condition; his temperature was exactly what it had been throughout the preceding fortnight. I carefully wiped the clinical thermometer, and replaced it in its case. As I did so, I was startled by hearing a wild shriek in the hall outside. It was a woman's voice, and the accent was one of deadly terror. I should have recognised the voice anywhere: it was the Dona Consuelo's. What could have happened? Once more it rang out, and almost before I knew what I was doing I had rung the bell for Nikola, and had rushed from the room into the hall outside. No one was to be seen there. I ran in the direction of the corridor which led towards the Dona's own quarters, but she was not there! I returned and followed that leading towards that terrible room behind the iron gate. The passage was in semi-darkness, but there was still sufficient light for me to see a body lying upon the floor. As I thought, it was the Dona Consuelo, and she had fainted. Picking her up in my arms, I carried her to the hall, where the meal of which I was to partake at the end of my watch was already prepared. To bathe her forehead was the work of a moment. She revived almost immediately.

"What is the matter?" she asked faintly. "What has happened?" But before I could reply, the recollection of what she had seen returned to her. A look of abject terror came into her face.

"Save me, save me, Dr. Ingleby!" she cried, clinging to my arm like a frightened child. "If I see them again, I shall go mad. It will kill me. You don't know how frightened I have been."

" Found herself standing before the open door of that demon-haunted room."

I thought I was in a position to understand exactly.

"Hush!" I answered. "Try to think of something else. You are quite safe with me. Nothing shall harm you here."

She covered her face with her hands, and her slender frame trembled under the violence of her emotion. Five minutes had elapsed before she was sufficiently recovered to tell me everything. For some days, as I soon discovered, she had been left almost entirely alone, and having nothing to occupy her mind, had been brooding over her enforced separation from her aged relative. The more she thought of him the more became her craving to see him, in order to convince herself that no harm had befallen him. A semi-hysterical condition must have ensued, for she rose from her bed, dressed herself, and, taking a candle in her hand, started in the hope of finding him. By some stroke of ill-fortune she must have discovered a passage leading to Ah-Win's portion of the castle, and at last found herself standing before the open door of that demon-haunted room.

"What does it all mean?" she cried piteously "What is this place, and why are these dreadful things here?"

I was about to reply, when the curtain at the end of the hall, covering the door of the laboratory, was drawn aside, and to my horrified amazement Nikola, who I imagined had taken my place in the patient's room, stood before us. As I saw him and realised the significance of the position, a cold sweat broke out upon my forehead. What construction would he be likely to place upon my presence there? For a few seconds he stood watching us, then an expression that I can only describe as being one of terror spread over his face.

"What does this mean?" he cried hoarsely. "What have you done?" Then running to the door of the Don's room, he drew back the curtain and entered. Leaving the Dona where she was, I followed with such fear in my heart as I had never known before. I found Nikola fumbling with the case of the clinical thermometer, and trembling like a leaf as he did so. Thrusting it into the old man's mouth, he hung over him and waited as if his whole life depended on the result. Withdrawing it again and holding it up to the light, he gazed at it.

"Too late!" he cried, and I scarcely recognised his voice, so changed was it. "His temperature has dropped a point! Ingleby, this is your doing. For all you know to the contrary, you may have killed him."

CHAPTER VII. LOVE REIGNS

IN the preceding chapter I made you acquainted with the calamity which befell our patient, and of the serious position in which I found myself placed with Nikola in consequence. While knowing in my own heart that I was quite innocent of any intentional neglect of duty, I had yet to remember that had I remained on watch, instead of leaving the room to ascertain what had befallen the Dona Consuelo, it would in all probability never have happened. On the other hand, I had signalled Nikola and called him to my assistance before abandoning my charge. How it was he had not answered my summons was more than I could understand. As it transpired afterwards, however, and as is usual in such things, the explanation was a very simple one. In the last chapter I said that when he left me to go to the laboratory, he was quite exhausted; he had eaten nothing for many hours, and as a natural result the fumes of the herbs he was distilling had overpowered him and he had fallen in a dead faint upon the floor.

As long as I live I shall retain the recollection of the next fourteen hours. During the whole of that time Nikola and I fought death inch by inch for the body of the old Don. From midnight until the following afternoon, neither of us crossed the threshold of the sick-chamber; and during the whole of that time, save to give me brief directions, Nikola spoke no word to me at all. It was only when the mercury in the clinical thermometer was once more established on its accustomed mark that he addressed me. Rearranging the bed-covering and wiping his clammy forehead with his pocket-handkerchief, he turned to me.

"I think he will do now," he said, "provided he does not lose ground within the next half-hour, we may take it for granted that he is out of danger."

This was the opportunity for which I was waiting: I accordingly seized it.

Dr. Nikola's Experiment

"I am afraid, Dr. Nikola," I said, mustering courage as I progressed, "that you consider me to blame for what has happened." He looked sharply at me, and then said coldly:

"I fail to see how I could very well think otherwise. I left you in charge, and you deserted your post."

"But I assure you," I continued, "that you are misjudging me. I could not help myself. I heard the girl scream, and ran to her assistance. At the same time I took care to ring the bell for you before I left the room."

"You should not have left it at all until I had joined you," he answered, still in the same icy tone. "As a matter of fact, I did not hear your summons; I had fainted. And one other question, What was the girl doing in this portion of the castle?"

"She was hysterical," I answered, "and was searching for her great-grandfather. She did not know, herself, how she got here; but, as ill-luck would have it, she saw your terrible people, and was frightened nearly to death in consequence.

"For common humanity's sake I could not leave her as she was. Having rung for you, I naturally thought you were with the Don, and that I was free to render her what assistance I could."

"Your argument is certainly plausible; but supposing the man had died during your absence? How would you have felt then?"

"I should have regretted it all my life," I answered. "But surely you must admit that would have been better than that a young girl should have been driven mad by fear."

"You do not seem to understand," Nikola replied, "that I would willingly sacrifice a thousand girls to accomplish the great object I have in view. No! no! Ingleby, you have been found wanting in your duty; you have checked the progress of the experiment, and if that old man had died"—here he took a step towards me, and his face

115

suddenly became livid with passion—"as I live at this moment you would never have seen the light of day again. I swear I would have killed you with as little compunction as I would have destroyed a dog who had bitten me."

So menacing was his attitude, and so fiendish the expression on his face, that I instinctively recoiled a step from him, and yet I don't think my worst enemy could accuse me of being a coward. Was the man a lunatic? I asked myself; had the magnitude of his discovery turned his head? If so, I must be careful in my dealings with him.

"I am afraid I do not understand you, Dr. Nikola," I said, trying to appear calmer than I felt. "You talk in an exaggerated fashion, and one which I cannot permit. I confess to being in a certain measure to blame for what has happened; but if you feel that you can no longer repose the trust in me that you once felt, I would rather resign my post with you, and leave your house at once."

For a moment I thought I had detected a sign of fear in his face. Then his manner changed completely.

"My dear Ingleby," he said, patting me on the shoulder and speaking in quite a different tone, "we are wrangling like a pair of schoolboys. If I hurt your feelings just now, I hope you will forgive me and ascribe it to my anxiety. For the last two days, as you are aware, I have been overwrought. When I stated that I considered you to blame, I said more than I meant; for, of course, I know that you had no intention of injuring our patient, or of doing anything to prejudice the end we have in view. It was a combination of unfortunate circumstances, the ill-effects of which by good luck we have been able to remedy. Let us forget all about it."

"With all my heart," I said, with a momentary friendliness I had never felt for him before, and held out my hand to him. He took it, when to my surprise I found that his hand was as cold as ice. In this fashion the cloud between us appeared to have been blown away; but though it was no longer visible to the naked eye, it still existed, for I was unable to dispel from my mind the recollection of the threat he had used to me. If he were not in earnest now, he had at least been so then; and, for my own part, I put more faith in his threats than in his protestations of friendship.

"Come, come, this will never do," said Nikola, after the few moments' silence which had followed after our reconciliation. "It is nearly three o'clock. You had better go to your room and rest for a couple of hours, after which you can relieve me."

Seeing his haggard and weary face, I offered to remain on duty while he went to lie down, but to this he would not consent. It was plain he was still brooding over what had happened, and that he did not intend to trust me any further than he was absolutely obliged. Accordingly, I did not press him; but, as soon as I had noted the various temperatures, and had done what I could to help him, I left him to his vigil and went to my own apartment. I had had nineteen hours in the sick-room, and in consequence was completely worn out. During that time I had heard nothing of the Dona Consuelo. But when I laid my head upon my pillow and closed my eyes, her terrified face, as I had seen it the previous night, rose before me. Even then I could feel the thrill which had run through me as I took that lovely body in my arms. What place was this terrible castle, I asked myself, for such a woman? How dreary was the life she was compelled to lead in it; without companions, and cut off from the one person who only a week before had been all her world to her. This suggested another and a sweeter thought to me. Was there only one person she loved? I remembered how she had clung to me in the hall, and how she had appealed to me to save her. The mere thought that there might be something more than simple liking in her attitude was sufficient to set my heart beating like a sledge-hammer. Was it possible I could be falling in love? I, who had thought myself done with that sort of thing for ever? I smiled at the idea. A nice sort of position I was in to contemplate such a thing. And yet I was so lonely in the world that it soothed me to think there might be some one to whom I was a little more than the average man, and that that some one was a beautiful and noble woman. With these thoughts in my brain I fell asleep. A moment later, so it seemed, the electric bell above my head brought me wide awake again. One glance at my watch was sufficient, however, to show me that I had been asleep two hours. I dressed as quickly as possible and returned to the Don's room, when, much to my relief, Nikola informed me that there had been no relapse, and that all was progressing as satisfactorily as he could wish. Bidding me exercise the greatest vigilance, he left me and staggered from the room.

"A little more of this sort of thing, my friend," I said to myself, as I watched him pass out of the door—"only a little more, and you will be unfit for anything."

But I had yet to learn the strength of Nikola's constitution. He was like a steel bow: he might often be bent, but never broken.

It was not until the following morning that I saw Dona Consuelo again. We met upon the battlements as usual.

"Dr. Ingleby," she said, after we had been standing together some time, "I feel there is something I should say to you. I want to tell you how sorry I am for what occurred the other night. But for my folly in wandering about the castle as I did, I should not have seen"—she paused for a moment, and a shudder swept over her at the recollection. "I should not have seen what I did, and you would not have got into trouble with Dr. Nikola."

"But how did you know that I did get into trouble with Nikola?" I asked.

"Because Dr. Nikola spoke to me about it," she replied.

On hearing this, I pricked up my ears. Had Nikola taken her to task for what she had done?

In all probability he had blamed her. I tried to catch her on this point, but she would tell me nothing.

"You will accept my apology, won't you?" she asked; "it has made me so unhappy."

"You must not apologise to me at all," I answered; "I assure you none is needed. I would have given anything to have prevented your seeing—well, what you did, and still more to have prevented Nikola from speaking to you. He had no right to do so." Then, drawing a little closer to her, I took her hand: "Dona Consuelo," I said, "I am very much afraid your life here is a very unhappy one."

"I was happier in Spain," she answered. "But I do not want you to think that I am grumbling; you have given me your promise that no ill shall befall my great-grandfather, and for this reason I have no fear. If he is well, what right have I to complain of anything that may happen to myself? Some day perhaps Dr. Nikola will allow us to go back to Spain, and then I shall forget all about this terrible castle."

I wondered if the hope she entertained would ever be realised. But I was not going to permit her to suppose that I entertained any doubt at all about it. I felt I should like to have said more, but prudence restrained me. She looked so beautiful that the temptation was almost more than I could withstand. Whether she knew anything of what was in my mind, I cannot say; but somehow I fancied she must have done so, for, though I have no desire to appear conceited, I could not help thinking, when we bade each other goodbye, there was a look of sorrow in her face. Once more a fortnight went by. A month had now elapsed since our arrival at the castle, and, as I could plainly see, Nikola's experiment was at length achieving a definite result. The changes effected by the use of the electric batteries and the constant anointing which I have already described having ceased within a short time of the removal of the means by which they were occasioned, were now almost permanent, and were becoming more so every day. The patient's flesh was firmer and his skin was more elastic, while his usual pallor had given place to what might almost be described as a healthy tint. So far success had crowned Nikola's endeavours; but whether the final result would be what he desired was more than I could say. After the little *contretemps* which followed my mistake, already described, Nikola and I had agreed fairly well together. I was aware, however, that he was suspicious of my intimacy with the old Don's great-granddaughter; and from the way in which he glanced at the patient and the various instruments whenever he relieved me in the sick-room, I could tell that he was always anxious to satisfy himself that I had not done anything to prejudice the work he had in hand. It may easily be supposed therefore, that our partnership was far from being as pleasant as it had promised in London to be. To live in an atmosphere of continual suspicion is unpleasant at any time, but it becomes doubly so when another's happiness depends in a very large measure upon it. Of course, the reason was apparent to me; but there must have been something more in Nikola's mind than I could fathom, for I think I can assert most truthfully that never for a moment did I allow an effort to be wanting on my part to show how much I had his interest at heart. There was yet another thing which puzzled me. It was this: what was to happen when the required result had been achieved, and the old Don was transformed into a young man again? And more important still, what would become of his great-granddaughter? The whole thing seemed so absurd—so unnatural—if you like it better—that I could see no proper conclusion to it. Still, there was time to talk of that later on. The old Don was already, I am prepared to admit, in a certain sense, younger; that is to say, he did not present that appearance of great age which had been noticeable on board the *Dona Mercedes;* at the same time, he was still very far from being a young man.

One day I found sufficient courage to speak on this point to Nikola.

"That is one of the most remarkable points in my argument," he answered. "If he were to change his state so quickly, I should despair of success. As it is, I am more than hopeful, I am sanguine. To-morrow, if he continues to progress so favourably, we shall enter upon the third stage of the experiment. Granted that is successful, I shall be within measurable distance of the greatest medical discovery of this or any other century."

Knowing it was useless attempting to question him further, I was compelled to possess my soul in patience until the time should arrive for him to enlighten me. The following morning, as soon as I had finished my period of duty in the Don's chamber, I informed Nikola of my intention of going for a short stroll. The time, he had decided, was not ripe yet for the third phase; and as I knew that I should be kept closely employed as soon as it was, I was anxious to obtain as much exercise as possible while I had the opportunity. Accordingly, I placed my hat upon my head and descended to the courtyard. Strangely enough it was the first time I had set foot in it since our arrival at the castle. It was an exquisite morning for walking, and the sky was blue overhead, a brisk breeze was blowing, and when I had crossed the drawbridge and looked down into the little bay where the waves rolled in and broke with a noise like thunder upon the beach, I felt happier than I had done for some considerable time past. I watched the white gulls wheeling above my head, and as I did so the recollection of the time when I had last seen them rose before my mind's eye. It was the day that I had come so near speaking words of love to Dona Consuelo upon the battlements. I remembered the look I had seen on her sweet face, and as I did so I realised how much she was to me. With a light step and a feeling of elation in my heart, I made my way down the path towards the beach. Not a soul was to be seen, for I remembered having heard Nikola say that the yacht had gone south for stores. Reaching the water's edge, I stood and looked back at the castle. It was a sombre enough place in all conscience, and yet there was something about it now which affected me in a manner I can scarce describe. I looked at it for a few moments, and then, turning my back upon it, I set off along the beach at a brisk pace, whistling gaily as I went. Eventually I reached the further side of the bay, opposite that on which the castle was situated. Here the sand gave place to large rocks, which in their turn terminated in a tall headland. The view from these rocks was grand in the extreme. Night and day the rollers of the North Sea broke upon them, throwing showers of spray high into the air. Clambering up, I struggled for fifty yards or so, and finally seating myself upon a rock somewhat larger than the rest, prepared to enjoy the view. A surprise was in store for me. Looking back upon the way I had come, I caught sight of a figure walking towards me on the sands. Needless to say, it was the Dona Consuelo. Whether she was aware of my presence upon the rocks, I cannot say; I only know that as soon as I saw her I rose from where I was sitting and hastened to meet her. How beautiful she looked, and how her face lighted up as I came closer, are things which I must leave to the imagination of my reader.

" A Figure walking on the sands."

"You are further abroad than usual to-day, are you not?" I said, as we shook hands.

"Might I not say the same of you?" she answered with a smile. "The morning was so beautiful that I could not remain in that terrible old building. Every corner seems to suggest unhappy memories to me."

"Do you really think all the memories connected with it will be unpleasant?" I inquired.

She looked up at me in a little startled way, and blushed divinely as she did so.

"Could you expect me to regard the time I have spent in it with any sort of pleasure?" she inquired, fencing with my meaning, and giving me a Roland for an Oliver. "Only think what I have suffered in it!"

By this time we were strolling back together towards the rocks I have already described. The beach at this point narrowed considerably, and for some reason or another we walked a little nearer the cliff than I had done. Suddenly my companion stopped, and, pointing to the sand, said:

"You had a companion this morning?"

"I? I had no companion," I answered. "What makes you think so?"

"Look here," she said, and as she spoke she pointed to some footmarks on the sand before us.

"As you went up the beach you walked near the water's edge, and as you came to meet me you passed midway between your former tracks and the cliff. If you did not have a companion, whose footprints are these? They must have been made this morning, for, as you are aware, when the tide is full, it comes right up to the cliffs, and would be certain to wash out anything that existed before."

123

I stooped and examined the tracks carefully before I answered. They were evidently those of a man, and from the fact that the sand was hard the outline could be plainly distinguished. The foot that was responsible for them was a large one, and must have been clad in an exceedingly clumsy boot.

"I don't know what to think of it," I said. "One thing, however, is quite certain: I had no companion this morning. What about the old man and his wife at the castle?"

"I happen to know that they have both been hard at work all the morning," she answered. "Besides, what object could they have in following you? The beach leads nowhere, and from here to yonder point there is no place where you can reach the land above."

I shook my head. The problem was too much for me. At the same time I must own it disquieted me strangely. Who was this mysterious person who had dogged my footsteps? and what could have been his object in following me? For a moment I inclined to the belief that it might have been Dr. Nikola, who was anxious to discover how I spent my leisure. But on second thoughts the absurdity of the idea became apparent to me. But if it were not Nikola, who could it have been?

On reaching the rocks we seated ourselves, and fell to criticising the picture spread out before our gaze. There was something in my companion's manner this morning which, analyse it as I would, I could not understand. She was by turns light-hearted and sad; the two expressions chased each other across her face like clouds across an April sky. At last she returned to the topic which I knew must come sooner or later—that of her great-grandfather's condition.

"I seem cut off from him for ever," she said with infinite sadness. "I hear nothing of him from week's end to week's end, and I see nothing of him. He is gone completely out of my life."

" 'Look here!' she said."

"But only for the time being," I answered. "Dr. Nikola has assured you that he will restore him to health and strength. Think what that will mean, and how happy you will be together then."

"I know it is very wrong of me to say so," she continued; "but I cannot keep it back, Dr. Ingleby—I distrust Dr. Nikola. He is deceiving me; of that I feel sure."

Knowing what I did, I could not contradict her; but I saw my opportunity, and acted upon it.

"But if you do not trust Dr. Nikola," I said, "am I to suppose that you do not trust me?"

She was silent, and I noticed that she turned her face away from me, as if she were anxious to study the castle and the cliff. What was more, I noticed that her hand trembled a little as it rested on the rock beside me.

Once more I put the question, and as I did so, I leant a little towards her.

"I do trust you," she answered, but so softly that I could scarcely hear it.

"Consuelo," I said, in a voice but little louder than that in which she had addressed me, "you cannot think what happiness it is to me to hear you say that. As I have tried to show you, there is nothing I would not do to prove how anxious I am to be worthy of your trust. We have known each other but little longer than a month. In that time, however, I have learnt to know you as well as any man could know a woman. I have learnt more than that, Consuelo; I have learnt to love you better than life itself."

"No, no," she answered, "you must not say that. I cannot hear you."

"But it must be said," I answered. "My love will not be denied. You do love me, Consuelo; I can see it in your face. Don't you think that I watched and longed for it?"

Instead of turning her face to me, she turned it still further from me.

I took her little hand in mine.

"What is your answer, Consuelo?" I asked. "Be brave and tell me, darling."

"If I were brave," she said, "I should tell you that what you ask must never be. That it is hopeless—impossible. That it would be madness for us to think of such a thing. But I am not brave. I am so lonely in the world, and have lost so much that I cannot lose you also."

"Then you love me!" I cried, in such triumph as I had never felt for anything else in my life before. "Thank God, thank God for that!"

"Yes, I love you," she answered; and the great waves breaking on the rocks seemed to echo the happiness we both were feeling.

Over the next half-hour I must draw a veil. By the end of that time it was necessary for me to think of returning to the castle. Nikola's watch would be up in an hour, and I knew it would not do for me to keep him waiting. I said as much to Consuelo, and we immediately rose and set out on our return. As I walked beside her, I would not have changed position with any living man, so happy was I. My peace of mind, however, was destined to be but short-lived. We had crossed the greater number of the rocks, and were approaching the sand once more, when I received a shock which I shall not forget as long as I can remember anything. Clambering over the sharp and slippery rocks was by no means an easy business. It was, however, delightful to hold my sweetheart's hand in the pretence of assisting her. Occasionally it became necessary for us to make considerable detours, and once I bade her remain where she was until I had climbed a somewhat bigger rock than usual in order to find out whether we could proceed that way. I had reached the top, and was about to extend my hand to her assistance, when something caused me to look behind me. Judge of my surprise and consternation at finding, in the hollow below me, a man crouching on the sand, watching me.

It was the Chinaman I had seen on board the Dona Mercedes, the man who had thrown the knife which had so nearly terminated Nikola's existence.

How I managed to retain my presence of mind at that trying moment, I find it difficult now to understand. I only know this, that I realised in a flash the fact that it would be madness to pretend to have seen him. Accordingly, I stood for a moment looking out to sea, and then with a laugh that must have sounded far from natural, I rejoined Consuelo on the rock below and chose another path towards the sands.

"What is the matter?" she inquired when we had proceeded a short distance. "Your face is quite pale."

"I did not feel very well for a moment," I answered, making use of the first excuse that occurred to me.

"I am afraid you are not telling me the truth," she answered. "I feel convinced something has frightened you. Can you not trust me?"

Under the circumstances I thought it would be better for me to make a clean breast of it.

"I will trust you," I answered. "The fact of the matter is, I have discovered an explanation for the footsteps you pointed out to me upon the beach. We are being followed. When I jumped on the top of that rock, I found a man lying on the other side of it."

"A man? Who could he have been, and why should he be spying upon us? Did you recognise him?"

"Perfectly; I should have known him anywhere."

"Then who was he?"

"The Chinaman we saw on board the steamer. The man who stole the drugs Nikola entrusted to my care."

"Do you mean the man who entered my cabin and bent over to look at me?" she cried in alarm.

I nodded, and threw a quick glance back over my shoulder to discover whether we were still being followed. I could see nothing, however, of the man; a circumstance which by no means allayed my anxiety.

"What do you think we had better do?" inquired Consuelo.

"Hasten home as fast as we can go, and tell Nikola," I answered. "It is imperative he should know at once."

We accordingly continued our walk at increased speed, every now and then throwing apprehensive glances behind us. It is possible some of my readers *may* regard it as an exhibition of cowardice on my part to have sought refuge in flight; but when all the circumstances connected with it are taken into consideration, I am sure every fair-minded person will acquit me of this charge. Had I been alone, it is possible I might have turned and risked an encounter with the man; but Consuelo being with me rendered such a course impossible. For the first time since we had known it, the grim old castle, perched up on the cliffs, seemed a desirable place, and it was with a feeling of profound relief that I led my sweetheart across the drawbridge, and was able to tell myself that, for the time being at least, she was safe. On reaching the hall, I found that I had still twenty minutes to spare. I had no desire, however, for further leisure. What I wanted was to see Nikola at once, in order to tell him my unpalatable news.

On entering the room, I found him engaged in taking the old man's temperature. He looked up at me as if he were surprised to see me return so soon, but said nothing until he had finished the work upon which he was engaged.

"I can see from your face that you have had a fright, and that you have something to say to me concerning it," he began, when he had returned the thermometer to its case. "Our friend Quong Ma has turned up again, I suppose?"

"How did you know it?" I asked: for I had no idea that he was aware of the man's appearance in the neighbourhood.

"I guessed it," he answered, with one of his peculiar smiles. "You are the possessor of a most expressive countenance. Consider for a moment, and you will understand how it is I am able to arrive at a conclusion so quickly. In the first place, you have been for a walk with the young lady whom you love and who loves you in return."

"Perhaps you saw me," I replied sharply, feeling myself blushing to the roots of my hair.

"I have not left this room," he answered. "There is a long black hair on your collar, which would not have been there if you had spent your liberty by yourself. The same thing tells me that you love her, and she loves you. As for the other matter, the caretaker and his wife have been busily employed in the castle all the morning, while Ah-Win never leaves his own portion of the premises. There is only one person outside the walls who could have put that expression into your face, and that person is Quong Ma. Am I right?"

"Quite right," I replied. "He followed me along the sands, and hid himself among the rocks. In recrossing them from the point, I, as nearly as possible, jumped on him."

"I am very glad you did not quite do so," he answered. "Had you experienced that misfortune, you would not have been here to tell the tale. But enough of him for the present. Take your place here and watch our patient. In an hour's time his temperature should have risen two points. When it has done so, give him ten drops of this fluid in twenty drops of distilled water. A profuse perspiration should result, which will herald the return of consciousness and the new life. In twenty-four hours he should not only be conscious, but on his way to the commencement of his second youth; in forty-eight the improvement should be firmly established; while in a week we should have him on his legs, a living, moving, thinking man, and of my own creation. Watch him, therefore, and whatever happens do not leave this room. Meanwhile, I will have the drawbridge raised, and if Quong Ma can leap the chasm, and make his way into the castle, well, all I can say is, he is a cleverer man than I take him to be."

With that, Nikola left me, and I sat down to watch beside the aged Don. Apart from my duty towards him, I had plenty to think about, and over and over again I found myself recalling the incidents of the morning. Consuelo loved me, and happen what might I would prove myself worthy of her love. At the end of the hour, as Nikola had predicted, the patient's temperature had risen two points. I accordingly measured out the stipulated quantity of the medicine he had placed in readiness for me, added the necessary quantity of water, and poured it into the old man's mouth. Then I sat myself down to wait. Slowly the hands of the clock upon the wall went round, and sixty minutes later, just as Nikola had prophesied, small beads of perspiration made their appearance upon his forehead. It was an exciting moment, and one for which we had been eagerly waiting. I immediately rang the bell for Nikola, and upon his arrival informed him of the fact.

"At last, at last," he whispered. "It is certain now that I have made no mistake. From this moment forward his progress should be assured. In a week you will be rewarded by a sight such as the eye of man has never yet seen. Be faithful to me, Ingleby, and I pledge my word your future with the woman you love is assured."

For the remainder of that day, and, indeed, until eleven o'clock on the morning following, there was but little change in the old Don's condition. The casual observer would have seen but little difference from the day on which I had first taken charge of him on board the steamer. To Nikola and myself, however, who had spent so much time with him, and who had noted every change, there was a difference so vast that it seemed almost incomprehensible.

My watch next morning was from four o'clock until eight. At eight I breakfasted, and afterwards repaired to the battlements above in the hope of meeting Consuelo. Since Nikola had ordered the drawbridge to be raised, we had been compelled to make this our meeting-place, and, as it happened, Consuelo was first at the rendezvous.

"You have good news for me!" she cried, after I had kissed her. "I can see it in your face. What is it? Does it concern my great-grandfather?"

"It does," I answered. "It concerns him inasmuch as I am able to tell you that what Nikola promised you should happen has in reality come to pass. Everything has been satisfactory beyond our wildest hopes."

"And do you mean that all need of anxiety is over?" she cried.

"I do not mean that exactly," I answered. "But I think it very possible we shall soon be able to say so. Nikola is certainly the most wonderful man upon this earth."

What she said in reply it would be vanity on my part to recall, and would be only another instance of the folly of lovers' talk. Let it suffice that for upwards of an hour our converse was of the sweetest description. Hand in hand we sat upon the battlements, looking out across the sunlit sea, and building our castles in the air. We were interrupted by Ah-Win, who suddenly made his appearance before us and beckoned me to follow him.

Bidding Consuelo good-bye, I followed the fellow to the hall, where he pointed to the old Don's room and left me. I found Nikola in a state of the wildest excitement.

" We were interrupted by Ah-Win."

"I sent for you because the crisis is close at hand," he whispered. "At any moment now I may know my fate. Little by little I have built up this worn-out frame, strengthening, renewing, revivifying, and now the object of my ambition is almost achieved. A thousand years ago the secret was guessed by a certain secret sect in Asia. After working a hundred years or more upon it they at length perfected it But by the law of their order only one man was permitted to derive any benefit from it. I obtained their secret—how it does not matter, added to it what I thought it lacked, and here is the result."

As he spoke a visible tremor ran over the form on the bed before us. The excitement was well-nigh unbearable. For the first time in more than thirty days, movement was to be detected, the eyelids flickered, the mouth twitched, and little by little the eyes opened. Nikola immediately stooped over him, and concentrated all his attention upon the pupils. Then, placing his fingertips so close that they almost touched the lashes, he drew them away again in long transverse passes.

"Do you know me?" he asked, in a voice that shook with emotion. Almost instantly the man replied:

"I know you."

"Do you suffer any pain?"

"I do not."

"Sleep then, rest and gain strength, and in two days from this hour wake again a strong man."

Once more he placed his hands before the patient's eyes, and as he drew them away the lids closed. Nikola bent over him and listened, and when he rose he nodded reassuringly to me.

"It is all right," he said. "His respiration is as even and unbroken as that of a sleeping child."

As usual, my watch that night was from eight o'clock until midnight. From the fact that Don Miguel continued to sleep as quietly as at the moment when Nikola had hypnotised him, it was neither as difficult nor as anxious as before. Nor was I altogether discontented with my lot. I was in love, and was loved in my turn; I was engaged in deeply interesting employment, which, should the experiment terminate successfully, would in all probability ensure my being able to start for a second time in my profession, and with an added knowledge that would bring me to the top of the tree at once. The room in which I sat was warm and comfortable; outside, however, a violent storm was raging. The rain and wind beat against the window in the hall with wildest fury. Now, ever since I had watched by the Don's bedside, I had made it my habit to carefully lock the door as soon as Nikola had left the room. On this particular occasion I had not departed from my custom. The hands of the clock on the wall stood at ten minutes past eleven, and I was reflecting that I should not be sorry when my watch was over, and I at liberty to retire to bed, when to my astonishment I saw the handle of the door slowly turn. At first I almost believed that my imagination was playing me a trick; but when the handle revolved and was afterwards turned again, I was satisfied that this was not the case. Who was the person on the other side? It would not be Ah-Win, for the reason that he had been particularly instructed on no account ever to touch the door; Consuelo would not venture into that portion of the castle again on any consideration whatsoever; while Nikola himself, being aware that I always kept it locked, would have knocked before attempting to enter. Whoever it was must have been satisfied that the task was a hopeless one. At any rate he desisted, and I heard no more of him. A few moments later the ventilator required my attention, and I was too busy to bestow any more thought upon the matter. Indeed, it was not until Nikola knocked upon the door and relieved me that it entered my mind again. It became apparent immediately that he attached more importance to the incident than I was inclined to do.

"It's very strange," he said, "but it accounts for one thing which I must confess has puzzled me."

"What is that?" I inquired.

"I will show you," he answered, and led the way to the hall. At the farther end, near the window, he paused and pointed to a mark upon the floor. Not being able to see it very distinctly, I went down upon my hands and knees.

"Do you know what it is?" asked Nikola.

"I do," I answered. "It is the print of a naked foot."

"Yes," said Nikola, "and that foot was wet. It was more than that." Here he took a magnifying glass from his pocket, and also went down upon his hands and knees. "The chimney leading from Ah-Win's room," he said, "is almost exactly above our heads. In consequence, as you may have noticed, the battlements at that point are invariably covered with smuts. The naked foot which made this

Dr. Nikola's Experiment

mark brought some of these particles with it, which tells us that there was only one way in which the owner could have come, and that was down a rope and through the window. Let us examine the window."

We did so, but, so far as I could see, there was nothing there to reward us. The rain was pelting down, and the wind blew as I had never heard it do before.

"The man, whoever he was, was certainly not deficient in pluck," said Nikola. "I shouldn't have called to lower myself over the battlements on a night like this."

"Are you sure that he did so lower himself?" I inquired.

"I am quite sure," Nikola answered. "How else could he have come? The old Don is safe for half an hour at least; get your revolver, I will get mine, and we will go upstairs in search of the intruder."

I did as he directed, but with no great willingness. As you may suppose, I was quite convinced as to the identity of the mysterious visitor; and knowing his proficiency in the art of knife-throwing, I had not the smallest desire to become better acquainted with him. However, I was not going to allow Nikola to think I was afraid; so, putting the best face I could upon it, I did as he directed, and having assured myself that my weapon was loaded in every chamber, followed him along the corridor, up the stone staircase, and so out on to the battlements above. Of all the storms in my experience, I think that particular one was certainly the worst. The rain beat in our faces, and so great was the strength of the wind that the very castle itself seemed to shake and tremble before it. Revolver in hand, expecting every moment to be confronted by the man of whom we were in search, I followed Nikola in the direction of the engine-room chimney. I knew very well for what he was looking. He thought he would find a rope there, but in this he was disappointed. Nor were we able to discover any traces of human beings. We searched the whole length of the battlements in vain, and at last were perforce compelled to give up the hunt as hopeless. Returning to the stairway

136

once more, we were about to descend, when I saw Nikola stoop and pick something up. Whatever it was, he said nothing to me until we had reached the light of the corridor below. Then he held it up for me to see. It was a grey felt hat, the same that I had seen upon the Chinaman's head that morning.

"Mark my words," said Nikola, "we shall have trouble with Quong Ma before very long."

CHAPTER VIII. THE RESULT OF THE EXPERIMENT

WHEN we had returned to the corridor below the battlements, after our search for the man who had lowered himself down to the window of the hall, Nikola brought with him the soft felt hat I had observed upon the head of that villainous Chinaman, Quong Ma, that morning. Though neither of us was altogether surprised at finding that he was the man we suspected of being in the castle, we were none the more pleased at having our suspicions confirmed. The thing which puzzled us most, however, was how he had obtained admission, seeing that he had not been in sight when I had entered the castle that morning, that I had informed Nikola of my meeting with him within five minutes of my arrival, and that the drawbridge had been raised, if not at once, certainly within a quarter of an hour of my making my report. And yet it was plain, since he had been upon the battlements, that he *was* in the castle, and that his being there boded no good was as apparent as his presence.

"I always knew they had original ideas," said Nikola, "but I had no idea they were as clever as this. We shall have to be very careful what we do for the future; for from what I know of them, they would stick at nothing. To-morrow morning we must search the castle from dungeon to turret."

"And if we find them?"

"In that case," said Nikola, "I fancy I know a way of dealing with them. Dona Consuelo locks her door at night, I suppose?"

I informed him that I had advised her to do so.

"It would be better that we should make certain," he answered, and, proceeding to the door in question, he softly turned the handle. It was securely fastened from the inside.

"It seems all right," said Nikola. "Now we will return to our own quarters, and make everything secure there."

We did as suggested, and when everything was made fast, securely locked the door in the corridor behind us. Reaching the hall once more, we made a careful survey of the various rooms, including not only the apartments leading out of it, but also the passage leading to Ah-Win's quarters. No sign, however, of the man we wanted was to be seen there. Returning to the hall, we assured ourselves that our patient was still sleeping quietly, and then I bade Nikola good-night, and prepared to go to my room.

"I should advise you to lock your door," he said, as we parted. "You cannot take too many precautions when Quong Ma and his companion are about. Should I require your assistance during the night, I will ring for you."

I promised to answer his call immediately, and was about to turn away, when it occurred to me to ask him a question to which he had promised me an answer upwards of a month before.

"On the night that we left Newcastle," I said, "you were kind enough to say that when a fitting opportunity occurred you would tell me what has induced these men to follow you as they are doing."

"There is no reason why you should not hear," Nikola replied. "To tell it in full, however, would be too long a story, but I will briefly summarise it for you. In order to obtain the information necessary for carrying out the experiment upon which we are now engaged, I penetrated, as I think I have already informed you, into a certain monastery situated in the least known portion of Thibet. My companion and I carried our lives in our hands if ever men have done so in the history of the world. The better to carry out my scheme, I might explain, I impersonated a high official who had lately been elected one of the rulers of the order. At a most unfortunate moment the fraud was discovered, and my companion and I were ordered to be hurled from the roof of the monastery into the precipice below. We managed to escape, however, but not before I had secured the precious secret for which I had risked so much. The monks traced us on our journey back to civilisation, and two of the order, who have had special experience in this sort of work, were detailed to follow us, in the hope that they might not only regain possession of a book which contained the secret, but at the same time revenge the insult which had been offered to them."

"And you still have that book?"

"Would you care to see it?" asked Nikola.

I replied that I should like to immensely, whereupon he retired to his own apartment, to presently return bringing with him a small packet, which he placed upon the table. Untying the string which bound it, and removing a sheet of thin leather, he exposed to my gaze a small book, possibly eight inches long by four wide. The materials in which it was bound were almost dropping apart with age; the backs and corners, however, were clamped with rusty iron. The interior was filled with writing in the Sanskrit character, a great deal of which had faded and was barely decipherable. I took it tenderly in my hands.

"And it is to regain possession of this book that these men are following you?" I asked.

"To do that," he answered, "and to punish me for the trick I played them. They have not, however, accomplished their task yet; nor shall they do so if I can help it. Let me once get hold of Quong Ma, and he'll do no more mischief for some time to come."

As Nikola said this, his great cat, which for the past few moments had been sitting upon his knees, suddenly stood up, and, placing its forepaws upon the table, scratched at the cloth. Nikola was watching my face, and what he saw there must have considerably amused him.

"You are thinking that Apollyon and I are not unlike. When we get out our claws, we are dangerous. It would be well for our Chinese friend if he understood as much. Now you had better be off to bed, and I to my watch."

When Nikola relieved me at eight o'clock the morning following, it was plain that there was something important toward.

"Get your breakfast as soon as you can," he said, "and when you have done we will search the castle. You heard nothing suspicious during your watch, I suppose?"

"Nothing," I replied. "Everything has gone on just as usual."

As soon as I had finished my breakfast, Ah-Win was summoned, and together we set off on our errand. Beginning with the battlements, we took the castle corridor by corridor, floor by floor, examining every corner and staircase in which it would be possible for a human being to hide himself. Having exhausted the inhabited portion of the building, we searched the rooms into which no one had penetrated from year's end to year's end. These we also drew blank. Then descending another flight of stairs, we reached the basement, explored the great kitchens, once so busy, and now tenanted only by rats and beetles, and examined the various domestic offices, including the buttery and armoury, still without success. If Quong Ma was in the castle, it looked as if he must certainly possess the power of rendering himself invisible at will. At last we reached the keep, where the old couple who, as Nikola had said, officiated as caretakers during his absence, had their quarters. At the moment of our arrival the woman was bitterly upbraiding her husband for some misdeed.

"I tell 'ee," she was saying, slapping the table with her hand to emphasise her words, "that when I went to bed last night they vittals was in yonder cupboard. What I want 'ee to say is where they be now? Don't 'ee say 'ee never saw them, or that it was the cat as stole 'em, for 'ee may talk till 'ee be black in the face and I'll not believe 'ee. Cats don't turn handles and undo latches, and mutton don't walk out of the front door on its own leg. If 'ee be a man, 'ee'll tell the truth an' shame the devil."

I must leave you to picture for yourself the vehemence with which all this was said. The words poured from her mouth in a torrent, and every sentence was punctuated with slaps upon the table. So engaged were they in their quarrel that some moments elapsed before they perceived Nikola and myself standing in the doorway. When they did, the tumult ceased as if by magic.

"You seem to be enjoying yourselves," said Nikola drily; "perhaps you will be kind enough to tell me what it is all about."

He had no sooner finished than the irate old lady recommenced.

"It's just this way, my lord," she said, though why she should have bestowed a title upon Nikola I could not understand. "Last night I was troubled with the rheumatiz mortal bad, and went to bed early. My old man there, beggin' your pardon for the liberty I'm takin', was a-sittin' by the fire smokin' his pipe, such bein' his custom of an evening. He had had his supper, and as I se'd with my own eyes when he'd a finished there was the end of a leg of mutton in yon cupboard. When I comes this mornin' to take it out for breakfast, *it's* gone, and with it the bread as I baked with my own hands but yesterday. And he stands there, savin' your presence, my lord, and wants I for to believe as how he's not touched it, and the latch of the cupboard down, as you can see for yourselves, honourable gentlemen both, with your own eyes. I've been married these three-and-forty years, and I don't know as how you will believe it, my lord — "

Seeing that she was getting up steam once more, Nikola held up his hand to her to be silent.

"What you tell me is very interesting," he said, fixing his dark eyes upon her; "but let me understand you properly. You say you went to bed leaving your husband smoking his pipe in this room. Before retiring you convinced yourself that the food which is now not forthcoming was in the cupboard. Is that so?"

"Yes, my lord, and honourable gentlemen both."

Then, addressing her husband, Nikola continued:

"I suppose you went to sleep over your pipe?" The question had to be repeated, and his wife had to admonish him with, "Speak up to his lordship like a man," before he could answer. Even then his reply was scarcely satisfactory; he thought he might have fallen asleep, but he was not at all sure upon the point. He admitted he was in the habit of doing so; and, as far as Nikola was concerned, this settled the matter.

"Quong Ma," he said, turning to me. "Now I understand where he gets his food from." Then, turning to the woman, he said, "Your husband is a heavy sleeper, I suppose?"

"Why, bless you, sir," she replied, "he sleeps that heavy you can't wake him. And, as for snoring, why, the rattling of that old bridge out yonder, when they're a-drawin' of it up, ain't to be compared with him, as the sayin' is. I did hear of a man, when I lived down Sunderland, as did snore so that, when he woke up, the folks next door sent in to ask him to go on again, the stillness bein' that lonesome that they couldn't bear it."

Nikola peremptorily bade the old woman be silent, and ordered her for the future to see that her door was locked at dusk every evening. Then, addressing her husband, he inquired if the latter was conversant with the subterranean passages of the castle, and when he had replied in the affirmative, bade him light a lantern, and show us all he could. The man did so, and having conducted us across the courtyard, entered a long, low chamber, which might once have been used as a bakehouse. In this was a large wooden door, secured with many bolts, but now falling into considerable disrepair. These bolts he drew one by one with an air of importance that was indescribably comic.

"I don't quite understand how these bolts come to be fastened if the man is down below," said Nikola, addressing me. I shook my head, whereupon he bade the old man inform him whether there were any other entrances to the vaults in question.

143

"Lor', sir," the man replied, "the castle be fair mazed with them. If 'ee likes, I can take 'ee into most any room in the place from down below."

"I should have thought of that," said Nikola, more to himself than to me. "I am sorry I didn't question our friend here before. Quong Ma has evidently mastered the situation, and is playing a game of hide-and-seek. However, we'll examine the dungeons first, and the passages afterwards. So lead the way, my friend."

The old man going ahead carrying the lantern, Nikola following, and Ah-Win and myself bringing up the rear, we made our way down the clammy stone staircase into the subterranean portion of the castle. It was an experience that would have been worth anything to a novelist seeking colour for a historical tale; but knowing what I did about the man we were after, I cannot say that I appreciated the incident so much. In addition to my nervousness, my head was aching, while hot and cold perspirations alternately contributed to my general discomfort. What was the matter with me I could not think. As it was, I was the only member of the party, I believe, who felt any symptoms of fright. The old man with the lantern knew nothing of his danger. Ah-Win was an Asiatic and a fatalist, and in his master's presence appeared not to care whom or what he faced; while, as for Nikola himself, I believe most implicitly that cold-blooded individual would have faced certain death as coolly and contentedly as he would have tossed off a glass of wine. Lower and lower we descended, glancing into dungeons into which no light of day had ever penetrated, and stooping to make our way along passages in which the moisture from the roof fell drip, drip, drip, upon our heads. Search as we would, however, we could discover no trace of that villainous Celestial.

"We be close down alongside the sea now, your lordship," said the old man, "and when I tells 'ee that, I tells 'ee summat as not many folks as has bided in this 'ere castle ever knowed."

"Most admirable of men," said Nikola, "you are telling me exactly what I want to know. Do you mean that it's possible for us to reach the sea from where we are now standing without crossing the drawbridge?"

"That is exactly what I *do* mean, my lord," he answered. "And if your lordship and the honourable gentleman will come wi' I, I'll let 'ee see for your own selves."

Forthwith the old fellow, holding his lantern aloft, turned down a narrow passage, leading to the right, and a few minutes later brought us up to some steps, at the bottom of which the light of day could be plainly seen. To reach the bottom of the steps was the work of a moment, and once there a curious scene was revealed to us. The doorway opened into the chasm which I have described earlier, and was situated almost directly beneath the drawbridge and the keep. Kneeling down, Nikola and I looked over the edge and could plainly see a number of iron steps let into the rock one above the other. At the bottom—for it was now full tide—the sea washed and dashed with terrific force. Rising to his feet again, Nikola addressed the old man.

"Is it possible at low tide," he said, "to reach the sands from here?"

"Lor' bless you, yes, sir," the man replied. "When the tide is down, 'ee can get along from rock to rock without as much as wetting shoe leather."

"That accounts for everything," said Nikola with considerable satisfaction. "I understand exactly how Quong Ma got into the castle now; he must have laughed to himself when he saw that we had raised the drawbridge in the hope of keeping him out. However, forewarned is forearmed, and this place shall be bricked up this morning. You, my old friend, had better see to it, and be sure that you make a good job of it'"

The man promised to do so, and seeing that there was nothing further to be gained by remaining where we were, Nikola bade him conduct us back again to our own portion of the building by a secret passage if possible. The man assured us that he could do so, and was as good as his word. We climbed, crawled, and scrambled our way up the narrow steps and along a rabbit warren of a small passage behind our guide. At last he stopped.

"Would your lordship be kind enough to say where 'ee think 'ee are now?" he added.

"I have not the least notion," said Nikola.

"Nor I," I added.

"Well, sir, I will show 'ee," said the man, and after a little hunting he found and pressed something in the wall. There was a grating noise, a sound as of rusty hinges being slowly unfolded and then a portion of the wall swung outward and we found ourselves standing at the top of the great staircase within a few yards of Consuelo's apartments.

"This is uncanny, to say the least of it," remarked Nikola. "Pray do any of these interesting passages open into the young lady's room opposite, or into the smaller hall occupied by this gentleman and myself?"

"Not now, my lord," the man replied. "Time was when they did, but the old lord didn't take kindly to 'em, and they was bricked up as much as five year ago."

"I am glad to hear it," said Nikola; and you may imagine that I echoed the sentiment. Nikola thereupon thanked the old man and dismissed him, at the same time reiterating his order that the opening in the chasm below the drawbridge should be made secure.

The excitement of the search for Quong Ma and the damp of the passages had been too much for me, and by the time we reached the hall I could scarcely stand.

"Good heavens, Ingleby," said Nikola, as I dropped into a chair, "you're looking awfully ill. What is the matter?"

"I can't exactly say," I answered. "I fear I must have caught a chill on the battlements last night."

"And yet you accompanied me down to those damp passages this morning. Was that wise?"

"I was not going to let you go alone," I replied.

He glanced sharply at me, as if he would read my thoughts.

"Well, well, I'll tell you what you must do: you must be off to bed at once. There can be no doubt about that."

I tried to protest: I explained my desire to see the end of the experiment; but Nikola was adamant. To bed I must go, willy-nilly; and to bed I accordingly went, but not in my own room off the hall. An apartment farther down the corridor, next door to that occupied by Consuelo, was arranged for me; and when I was safely between the blankets, Nikola prescribed for me, and my sweetheart was duly installed as nurse. My indisposition must have been more severe than I had supposed, for before nightfall I was in a high state of fever, and by midnight was delirious.

I remember nothing further until I opened my eyes and found Consuelo sitting by my side.

"What does this mean?" I inquired, surprised to find her there.

"It means that you have been very ill," she answered, "and that I am your nurse, and am not going to permit you to talk very much."

To do this was a feat of which I was incapable, but I was not going to be silent until I had learnt something of what had happened.

"How long have I been ill?" I inquired.

"More than a week," she answered; and then added, "You naughty boy, you little know what a fright you have given me. But you must not talk any more, or Dr. Nikola will be angry."

She poured out some medicine for me, bade me drink it, and then reseated herself beside me. In five minutes I was wrapped in a heavy slumber, from which I did not wake for several hours. When I did, I found Dr. Nikola installed as nurse; Consuelo had disappeared.

"Well, Ingleby," said Nikola cheerily, as he felt my pulse, "you have had a sharp bout of it, but I am glad to see we have managed to pull you through. How do you feel in yourself?"

"Much better," I answered, "though still a bit shaky."

"I don't wonder at it," he said. "Do you feel hungry?"

"I feel as if I could eat anything," I answered.

"Well, that's a good sign. I'll see that something is sent you. In the meanwhile keep as quiet as possible. When I leave you, I'll send your sweetheart to you; she has been a devoted nurse, and between ourselves I rather fancy you owe your life to her."

"God bless her!" I answered fervently. "But you call her my sweetheart. What do you mean by that?"

"My dear fellow, I know everything. One night the young lady in question was rather concerned about you, and in her agitation she allowed the cat to slip out of the bag. You young people seem to have managed the matter pretty well in the short time you have known each other. Now keep quiet for a few moments while I see if I can find her."

He was making for the door, when I stopped him.

"You have not told me how the Don is," I said. "How does the experiment progress?"

His face clouded over.

"It has proved successful," he answered, but with a sudden sternness that surprised me. It was for all the world as if he were trying to convince me that what he said was correct, although in his own heart he knew it was not so. When he spoke again, it was very slowly.

"Yes, Ingleby," he said, as if he were weighing every word before he uttered it, "the experiment has proved a success. I have made the Don a young man, but—well, to tell the truth, I have made a mistake in my calculations—a mistake that I cannot explain and that I can in no way account for."

"And the result?"

"Don't ask me," he said, "for I am afraid I do not know myself. By the time you are on your feet again, I shall hope to have come nearer an understanding of the situation. Then I shall be able to tell you more of what I hope and fear. At present I scarcely like to think of it myself."

To my surprise, as I watched him, I saw great beads of perspiration start out upon his forehead, and, for the first time since I had known him, I saw a look of terror in Dr. Nikola's face. I tried to question him further upon the subject, but he bade me wait until I was stronger, and, presently repeating that he would find Consuelo, he left me. When my sweetheart entered the room, looking more beautiful than I had ever seen her, I forgot, for the time being, about Nikola.

"You are looking much better," she said, as she came toward me and put down upon the table the tray she carried in her hand. "Here is some beef-tea which I have made for you myself. If you don't drink it *all* up, I shall let the old woman in the kitchen make it for you in the future and bring it to you herself."

"You had better not," I answered. "In that case, I should refuse to touch a drop of it, and should die of slow starvation in consequence."

With a gentleness that was infinitely becoming to her, she lifted my head and held the cup while I drank. If I took longer over it than I should have done at any other time, the fact must, of course, be attributed to my weakness.

"Dr. Nikola says he is very pleased with the progress you have made," she said, when she had replaced the cup upon the table. "But you are to be kept very quiet for some days, and to sleep as much as possible."

"And when am I to get up?" I asked.

"Get up!" she cried in mock horror. "You must not even think of such a thing for a week at least."

"A week!" I replied. "Do you think I've to stay here for a week?"

"So Dr. Nikola says."

The remainder of our conversation is too sacred to be set down in cold-drawn type. Let it suffice that, when I fell asleep again, it was with her hand in mine. I was more in love even than I had been before.

As Consuelo had predicted, more than a week had elapsed before I was permitted to leave my room. Even then I was not allowed to return to my duties at once, but spent the greater portion of my time with Consuelo on the battlements gaining strength with every breath of sea air that I inhaled.

Nikola I saw but little of. He examined me every morning, and on one or two occasions honoured us with his company for a brief period on the castle roof. At the best of times, however, he was not a good companion. He was invariably absorbed in his own thoughts, spoke but little, and struck me as being anxious to say goodbye almost as soon as he arrived. Since then I have learned the true reason of it all, and I have been able to see that complex character in a new light. It never struck me how lonely the man's life must be. During the whole time that I was associated with him I never once heard him speak of kith or kin. Friends he appeared to have none, while his acquaintances numbered only such men as were necessary to the particular work he happened to be engaged in at the moment of their meeting. His very attainments, his peculiar knowledge of the world, of its under and mystic side, were sufficient to make him hold aloof from his fellow-men. In all matters of comfort a rigid ascetic, the good things of life had no temptation for him. To sum it all up, of this I feel certain, so certain indeed that at times it becomes almost a pain, that Nikola, with all his sternness, his self-denial, his genius and his failings, hungered for one thing, and that was to be loved. Why should I say this, considering that the only evidence I have to offer tends to lead one's thoughts in a contrary direction? I do not know, but as I remarked just now, I feel convinced that my hypothesis is a correct one, as I am that I love Consuelo. But to return to my story. It was not until nearly a fortnight had elapsed, since my return to consciousness, that I was permitted to take up my duties again. When I did, I returned to my old quarters leading out of the hall, and I think Nikola was pleased to once more have my co-operation,—at any rate, he led me to suppose that he was.

"When you think you are up to the mark, I shall be pleased to show you the Don," he said, "and to hear your opinion of him."

I expressed myself as being quite equal to seeing him at once.

"Very good," he answered, "but I warn you to be prepared for a great and somewhat unpleasant change in the man."

So saying, he led me across the hall towards the room in which I had, before my illness, spent so many hours. Inserting the key in the lock, he turned it and we entered. I had expected to find it exactly as I had last seen it. A surprise, however, was in store for me. The bedplace in the centre was gone, as were both the electrical appliances. The clock and thermometers had been removed, the only things that still remained being the electric lights which were suspended from the ceiling and the enclosed fixtures for regulating the supply of hot and cold air. In point of fact, it was as bare a room as well could be imagined.

"Don Miguel," said Nikola, "I have brought an old friend to see you."

I looked about the room, but for a moment could see nothing of the old man in question. Then my eye lighted on what looked like a heap of clothes huddled up on a mattress in the corner. On hearing Nikola's voice, a face looked up at me—a face so terrible, so demoniacal I might say, that I involuntarily shrank from it. What there was about it that caused me such revulsion, I cannot say. It was the countenance of a young man, if you can imagine a man endowed with perpetual youth, and with that youth the cunning, the cruelty, and the vice of countless centuries.

"Steady, my friend," I heard Nikola say, and as he did so he placed his hand upon my arm. "Remember, Ingleby, this is nothing more than an experiment."

Then addressing the crouching figure, he bade him stand up. With a snarl like that of a dog, or rather of a wild beast, who is compelled to do a thing very much against his will, the man obeyed. I was able then to take better stock of him. Accustomed as I was to the old Don's face, I found it difficult to realise that the healthy, vigorous man standing before me was he, and yet I had only to look at him carefully to have all doubt upon the subject removed. He was the same and yet not the same. At any rate, he was an illustration of the marvellous, nay, the almost unbelievable, success of Nikola's experiment.

"You remember the Don as he was, and you can see to what I have been able to bring him," said Nikola sadly, and for one moment without a trace of triumph. This, however, was soon forthcoming.

"Out of an old man tottering on the brink of the grave, I have manufactured a young and vigorous creature such as you now see before you. I have made him, I have transformed him, I have subjected Nature to science, I have revolutionised the world, abolished death, and upset the teachings, and the essential idea, of all religions. I have proved that old age can be prevented, and the grave defied. And—*and—I have failed.*"

Under the intensity of his emotion his voice broke, and something very like a sob burst from him. Never since I had known Nikola had I seen him as he was then. To all appearances he was well-nigh broken-hearted.

"If you have done all this," I asked, "how can you say that you have failed?"

"Are you so blind that you cannot see?" he answered. "Examine the man for yourself, and you will find that he is a human being in animal life only. I have given him back his youth, his strength, his enjoyment in living, but I cannot give him back his mind. In his body I have triumphed; in his brain I have completely failed."

"But cannot this be set right?" I inquired. "Is the case quite hopeless?"

"Nothing is hopeless," he answered; "but it will take years, centuries perhaps, of work to find the secret. I thought, when I built up the body, I should be building up the brain as well. It was not so. In proportion as his body renewed its youth, his brain shrunk. Let me give you an illustration."

He went forward towards the man, who was now once more crouching upon the floor, watching us over his right shoulder, as if he were afraid we were going to do him harm.

"Well, Miguel," said Nikola, patting him upon the head, and speaking to him in the same tone he would have used to a favourite monkey, "how is it with you to-day?"

The man, however, took no notice, but bending down played with the lace of Nikola's shoe, now and again looking swiftly up into his face, as if he dreaded a blow, and as swiftly looking away again.

"This should prove to you what I mean," said Nikola, addressing me. "In his present condition he is less than a man, and yet where would you find a finer frame? His heart, his lungs, his constitution, all are perfect."

While he had been speaking, he had turned his back upon the beast upon the floor, and as he uttered the last words he moved towards me. He had not taken a step, however, before the Don was half on his feet. From childish idiocy his expression had changed until it was a fiendish malignity that surpasses all description in words.

In another moment he would have thrown himself on Nikola. As it was, he glared at him until he turned, when in an instant the wild expression had gone, and he was crouching upon the floor once more, picking at his fingers and smiling to himself.

"You can see for yourself what he is," said Nikola: "an imbecile; but for one ray of hope I should despair of him."

"There is, then, a ray of hope," I said eagerly, clutching like a drowning man at the straw he held out. "Thank God for that!"

"There is a ray," he answered, "but it is a very little one. I will give you an example."

Turning to the wretched creature on the floor, he extended his hand towards him, and, gradually lifting it, bade him rise. The effect was instantaneous. The man rose little by little until he stood upright Once more pointing his hand directly at him, Nikola moved towards him, until the points of his fingers were scarcely an inch from the other's eyes. Then, slowly raising his fingers, he made an upward and a downward pass.

The eyes closed, and yet the man still remained rigid against the wall. Turning to me, Nikola said:

"You can see for yourself that he is absolutely under my influence and control."

I approached and made a careful examination. There could be no doubt about his condition: it was one of hypnotic coma; and, on raising one of the eyelids, I found the ball turned upwards and wandering in its orbit.

"You are satisfied?" inquired Nikola.

"Perfectly," I answered.

"In that case let us proceed."

"To whom am I speaking?" asked Nikola, addressing the man before him.

"To Miguel de Moreno," was the answer, given in a perfectly clear and strong voice, and without apparent hesitation. "Do you know where you are?"

"I am with Dr. Nikola."

"Before you came to me, with whom and where did you live?"

"I lived with my great-granddaughter in Cadiz."

"Have you any recollection of coming to England?"

"I remember it perfectly."

"Now lie down upon that mattress, and sleep without waking until eight o'clock to-morrow morning."

The man did as he was ordered without hesitation. Nikola covered him with the blankets, and as soon as we had made sure of his safety, we left the room, carefully locking the door after us.

"You can have no idea, Ingleby, what a disappointment this has been to me. Three times before I have tried and failed, but this time I made sure I had success within my grasp. I have progressed farther now than I have ever done before, it is true; but it is the brain that has beaten me. As long as I live I will persevere, and the perfect man, who shall retain his youth through all ages, shall eventually walk the earth. Now good-night."

He held out his hand to me, and as I shook it Apollyon came up, and rubbed himself against my leg, as if to show that he too appreciated my sympathy. I was about to retire to my room, when it struck me that I had heard nothing of our friend Quong Ma since we had searched the subterranean portion of the castle for him. I asked Nikola if he had anything to tell me concerning him.

"Nothing," he answered, "save that last night I felt certain that I saw a man cross the courtyard. It was just before midnight, the moon was about the building, and I am ready to stake anything that I am not deceived."

"But who could it have been?"

"That's exactly what I want to know," he answered. "You were safe in bed and asleep. It was not the caretaker, for I tried his door and found it locked, and from the sound that greeted me I had good proof it was not he."

"But might it not have been Ah-Win?" I asked.

"I thought so, and before going in search of the figure I hastened to his room, only to find him also asleep."

"In that case it must have been Quong Ma. But how does the fellow live? and why does he not strike?"

156

"Because he has not yet found his opportunity. When he does, you may be sure he will avail himself of it. Now once more good-night You need not trouble about our patient; I shall take a look at him about midnight."

"Good-night," I said, and went to my room, the door of which I carefully locked. My last waking thoughts were of Consuelo, and my speculations as to what her feelings would be when she realised the terrible change that had taken place in her great-grandfather were sufficient to give me a nightmare. Over and over again I was afflicted with the most horrible dreams; and when I was roused by a loud thumping on my door, and Nikola's voice calling for admittance, it seemed so much part and parcel of the horror my brain had just pictured for me, that for the moment I took no notice of it. It sounded again; so, springing from my bed, I ran to the door, and opened it.

"What is the matter?" I asked, when he was standing before me. His usual pale face was now ghastly in its whiteness.

"Good heavens, man!" he cried, "you have no notion of what has happened. Dress yourself immediately and come with me!" He sat upon my bed while I huddled my clothes on; then, when I was ready, he seized me by the wrist, and half-dragged me, half-led me into the hall. Once there, he pointed to the figure of a man stretched out before his door. *It was Ah-Win; and his throat was cut from ear to ear!*

The sight was so sudden, and so totally unexpected, that it was almost too much for me. Recovering my presence of mind, however, I knelt down and examined him.

"Look at his hands!" said Nikola. "They are cut to the bone by some sharp-bladed instrument. The murderer must have come here in search of me. Ah-Win must have met him, tried to prevent him reaching the door, was unable to warn us, and so have met his fate."

We were both too much overcome to continue the discussion. *Quong Ma had struck at last!*

CHAPTER IX. WAR AND PEACE

AT the conclusion of the preceding chapter, I described to you the terrible discovery we had made of the death of Ah-Win. That he had met his fate in an endeavour to prevent Quong Ma from reaching his master's room seemed quite in accordance with the evidence before us. Small wonder was it, therefore, that Nikola was affected. But even in his grief he proved himself unlike the average man. Another man would have bewailed his loss, or at least have expressed some sorrow at his servant's unhappy lot. Nikola, however, did neither, and yet his grief was plain to the eye as if he had wept copious tears. Having satisfied himself that the poor fellow really was dead, he bade me help him carry the body down the passage to an empty room which adjoined his former quarters.

We laid it upon a bed there, and Nikola followed me into the passage, carefully locking the door behind him. When we were back in the hall once more, Nikola spoke.

"This has gone far enough," he said. "Come what may, we must find Quong Ma. The fellow must be in the castle at this minute."

"Shall we organise a search for him?" I said. "The man must be captured at any hazard; we are risking valuable lives by allowing him to remain at large."

Though I used the plural, I must confess I was thinking more of my darling than of anybody else. How did I know that, when Quong Ma found it impossible for him to get hold of Nikola, he would not revenge himself upon Consuelo?

"That we must find him goes without saying," Nikola replied. "I doubt very much, however, if it would be prudent for you to take part in the search. In the first place, you are still as weak as a baby; and in the second, the damp of the subterranean passages might very easily bring on a return of the fever."

"You surely do not imagine that I should permit you to go alone," I said.

Nikola gave a short laugh.

"I do not want to appear boastful," he said, "but I am very much afraid you do not know me yet, my dear Ingleby. However, I will confess that if you really do desire it, and feel equal to the exertion, I shall be very glad of your company."

"When do you propose to start?"

"At once," he answered. "I shall not know a minute's peace until I have revenged Ah-Win."

"And supposing we catch the fellow, what do you propose to do with him? It is a long way from here to the nearest police station."

"I don't fancy somehow I shall trouble the police," he said. "But we will talk of what we will do with him when we have got him. Now, if you are ready, come along."

Thereupon, for the second time we searched the castle for Quong Ma. As before, we first visited the battlements and the rooms on the next floor, the basement offices followed, and still being unsuccessful, we unbolted the door leading to the dungeons and entered the subterranean portion of the building. Cool as I endeavoured to appear, I am prepared to confess that, when the icy wind came up to greet us from those dark and dreary passages, I was far from feeling comfortable. I don't set up to be a braver man than my fellows, but it seemed to me to require more pluck to enter those dismal regions than to take part in a forlorn hope. With our revolvers in our hands, and Nikola holding the lantern above his head, we explored passage after passage and dungeon after dungeon. Rats scuttled away from beneath our feet, bats flew in the darkness above our heads; but, as before, not a sign of Quong Ma.

"I cannot understand it," said Nikola at last, and his voice echoed along the rocky passages. "We have explored every room in the castle and every dungeon underneath it, and not a trace of the man can we discover. We have bricked up the opening into the chasm, and lifted the drawbridge that connects us with the outside world, and yet we cannot catch him. He must be here somewhere."

"Exactly; but where?"

"If I knew, do you think I should be standing here?" Nikola replied sharply. "But let us try back again. I want to explore that secret passage the old man showed us the other day. I remember now that there was something that struck me as being rather peculiar about it."

We accordingly retraced our steps, found the passage in question, and ascended it. Reaching the point where, on the previous occasion, we had turned off to find the trap-door, opening at the head on the great staircase, we found, as Nikola had supposed, a second and smaller turning half hidden in shadow and which bore away to the right, that is to say in the direction of the keep. Fortunately, it was now level going, but so narrow was the passage that it was still impossible to walk two abreast.

"Hark! what was that?" Nikola suddenly cried, stopping and holding the lantern above his head.

We stopped and listened, and sure enough a shuffling noise came from the passage in front. A moment later the same sound we had heard when the old caretaker had opened the secret door reached us.

"If I am not mistaken, we have found his lair at last," my companion shouted and ran forward.

But certain as we felt that it was Quong Ma we had heard, we were too late to convince ourselves of the fact. The secret door stood open; the man, however, was not to be seen in the passage outside.

"Where are we?" I asked, for I was not familiar with the corridor in which we found ourselves.

"Between the keep and Ah-Win's quarters," Nikola replied. "Now I understand how that fiend has found his way into the hall. But let me think for a moment: there is the gate between us and the hall, and I have the key in my pocket. There is no other exit in either direction, so it seems to me that we have got our man at last. Is your revolver ready?"

"Quite ready," I replied.

"Come along, then. But remember this: if he attacks you, show him no mercy. He'll show you none. Remember Ah-Win."

With that we made our way along the corridor in the direction of the room where Nikola's—well, where the murdered man had been quartered.

Nikola unlocked the door and looked in, while I remained in the passage outside. I really believe I was more afraid of what I should see in there than of Quong Ma himself.

"He is not there," said Nikola when he rejoined me, and then went to the gate and tested it. "And he can't get out here. We've missed him somewhere, and must look back again."

We accordingly retraced our steps, examining room by room and preparing ourselves every time lest, when we turned the handle, Quong Ma should jump out upon us. But in every case we were disappointed.

"I was surprised just now," said Nikola, after we had left the last apartment and stood in the corridor once more, "but I am doubly so now. What on earth can have become of the fellow? He seems to vanish into thin air every time we get near him. There must be another secret passage hereabout of which we are ignorant. Before we return, however, I want to make quite certain of one thing; let us continue that passage by which we ascended from the dungeons just now."

We did so, Nikola once more going ahead with the lantern.

"Just as I thought," he cried. "Look here!"

He stopped, and stood with his back to the wall. At this point the passage came to an abrupt termination, and on the floor before us was an old blanket, a quantity of straw, about a loaf and a half of bread, and an earthenware pipkin containing a quart or so of water. Under the blanket was a half-used packet of candles, and from the grease that bespattered everything it was easily seen how he had obtained his illumination.

"We have found our bird's nest at last," said Nikola, "but I am afraid we have driven him away from it for good and all. But we will have him yet, or my name's not Nikola. Now let us go back to the hall; we can do no good by staying here."

We returned, but not before we had taken possession of the things we had found, and had carefully marked the position of the secret door, in case we should want to use it again.

"After breakfast we will have another try," said Nikola. "In the meantime we had better take a little rest. You look as if you stood in need of it."

It would have been better for me had I abandoned any thought of such a thing, for with Ah-Win lying dead only a few yards away and Quong Ma still at large, the drowsy god was difficult, if not impossible, to woo. Every danger that it would be possible for a man to imagine, I pictured for Consuelo; and when at last I did fall asleep, the dreams that harassed me were of the most horrible description. Right glad was I when morning broke and it became necessary to attend to the duties of the day.

"If I were you, I should say nothing to your sweetheart either of her great-grandfather's condition or of the tragedy of last night," said Nikola. I agreed with him, although I knew that it could not be very long before the former would become known to Consuelo.

"But surely she will hear about Ah-Win before very long?" I said. "Will it not be necessary for you to communicate with the county police, and for an inquest to be held?"

"Ingleby," replied Nikola, "ask me no questions I have no desire to draw you into the matter. It is sufficient for you to know that Ah-Win is dead,"—he paused for a minute, and then added, significantly—"*and buried!*"

Try how I would, I could not contain my surprise. How, when, and by whom had the poor Chinaman been buried? Had Nikola carried it out himself? It seemed impossible, and yet, knowing as I did the indomitable energy and working powers of the man, I felt it might very well be true. I would have questioned him further, but I could see that he was not in the humour to permit it. For this reason I held my peace, though I knew full well at the time that by so doing I was giving my consent to what was undoubtedly an illegal act.

From what I have said, I fancy it will be readily agreed that the past two or three days had been as full of incident as the greatest craver after excitement could desire. I had recovered from a serious illness, had witnessed the result of one of the most extraordinary experiments the world had seen, Ah-Win had been murdered, we had discovered Quong Ma's hiding-place in the castle, and had had a most exciting chase after him. Now Ah-Win had been buried secretly by Nikola, and if what had been done was discovered by the authorities, there is no saying in what sort of trouble we might not find ourselves. As soon as we had seen the Don, who was still wrapped in the same hypnotic slumber, and had breakfasted, we organised another search, only to meet with the same result. Later, I spent an hour with Consuelo upon the battlements. I was careful, however, to tell her nothing of the death of Ah-Win, nor of the reappearance of the detestable Chinaman in the castle. It would have served no good purpose, and would only have frightened her needlessly. When she reiterated her desire to see her great-grandfather, I found myself, if possible, at a still greater disadvantage. On returning to Nikola in the hall, I placed the matter before him. To my surprise, he did not receive it in the same spirit as I had expected he would do. I had anticipated a direct refusal, but he gave me nothing of the kind.

"Why should she not see him?" he said. "Provided she give me proper notice, I fancy I can arrange that he shall behave in every way as she would wish him to do."

"When, then, may the interview take place?"

"Let us say at midday. Will that suit you? But before we arrange anything definitely, let us examine him ourselves, and see how he is likely to conduct himself."

We accordingly made our way to the patient's room. I had noticed by the hall clock that it wanted only three minutes of the hour at which Nikola had ordered the Don to wake. On approaching his bedplace, we found him still sleeping peacefully, in exactly the same position as when we had seen him last. With his eyes closed and one strong arm thrown out upon the floor, he looked a magnificent specimen of a man. If only Dr. Nikola could perfect the brain, here was a being seemingly capable of anything. But would he be able to do so? That was the question. Watch in hand, Nikola knelt down beside the bed, and for some time not a sound broke the stillness of the room. Punctually, however, as the long hand of the clock pointed to the hour, the Don gave a long sigh. I jumped to the conclusion that he was about to wake in obedience to Nikola's command; but, to our surprise, he did not do so.

"Strange," I heard Nikola mutter to himself, and, stooping over the patient, he lifted the eyelids and carefully examined the pupils.

Five minutes went by, and still he did not wake.

" I threw myself upon the man."

"Don Miguel," said Nikola at last, "I command you to wake. You cannot disobey me,"

A slight movement was visible, but still the sleeper did not comply with the order given him. It was not until a quarter of an hour had elapsed that consciousness returned to him. With the opening of his eyes the animal look which I had noticed on the previous day came back to him. Instead of rising to his feet as he was ordered, he crouched and cowered in the corner, pulling at his bedclothes, and watching us the while, as if he would do us a mischief on the slightest provocation. Dangerous as the man had appeared the day before, it struck me that he was even more so to-day.

"It is very plain that we shall have to keep an eye on you, my friend," said Nikola. "I am not quite certain that you are going to be docile much longer. Let me feel your pulse."

He stooped, and was about to take hold of the other's wrist, when the man sprang forward, and, seizing the Doctor with both hands, laid hold of his arm with his teeth, just below the elbow. Fortunately, Nikola was wearing a thick velvet coat, otherwise the injury might have been a severe one. Seeing what had happened, I threw myself upon the man, and, tearing him off, forced him down upon his bed. He struggled in my grasp, snapping at me and foaming at the mouth like a mad dog; but I had him too secure, and did not let go my hold until Nikola had fixed his arms behind him.

"Good heavens, Nikola!" I cried, scarcely able to contain my emotion, "this is too terrible! What on earth are we to do with him?"

"I do not quite see what we can do," Nikola replied, wiping the perspiration from his forehead as he spoke. "However, I must try my hand on him once more. If you can manage to keep him still, and I can get him under my influence, we ought to be able to keep him quiet while we have time to think."

I did as requested, while Nikola made slow mesmeric passes before the man's eyes. It was fully ten minutes, however, before he succeeded; but as soon as he did, the patient's heartrending struggles ceased, and he lay down upon his bed, sleeping quietly.

"I began to be afraid I was losing my influence over him," said Nikola, as he rose to his feet.

"One thing is quite certain," I answered, "and that is, Consuelo must not see him while he is in this state. It would frighten her to death."

"And she would never forgive me," said Nikola; and I thought I detected a note of sadness in his voice. "Are you going to leave him as he is?" I inquired.

"For the present," Nikola answered. "I must make up something that will have a soothing effect upon him. You need have no fear; he will be quite safe where he is."

The words were scarcely out of his mouth before a movement on the bed caused us both to look round. Little as we had anticipated such a thing, Nikola's influence was slowly but surely working off, and the man was returning to his old state again. Even now, I never like to think of what happened during the next ten minutes.

Before we could reach him, the Don was on his feet and had rushed upon me, Nikola ran to my assistance, and, strong men as we both were, I assure you that at first we could not cope with him. The struggle was a terrific one. He fought like the madman he certainly was, and with an animal ferocity that rendered him doubly difficult to deal with. When, at last, we did manage to force him back on to his bed and make him secure, we were both completely exhausted; we could only lean against the wall and pant: conversation was out of the question.

"This will never do," said Nikola, when he had sufficiently recovered to speak; "if this sort of thing goes on, he will murder some one."

"But how are you going to prevent it?" I asked. "It is plain that your influence has lost its effect."

"There is nothing for it but to administer an opiate," he answered. "Do you think you can manage to hold him while I procure one?"

I fancied I could; at any rate, I expressed myself as very willing to try. Nikola immediately hurried away. He informed me afterwards that he was not gone more than a minute, but had I been asked I should have put the time down as at least a quarter of an hour. To describe to you my feelings during that wait would be impossible; the loathing, the horror, and the abject personal fear of the man writhing below me seemed to fill my whole being.

"I don't think we shall have very much more trouble with him for an hour or two to come," said Nikola, when the drug had taken effect, and we were on our feet once more.

"But we cannot go on administering drugs for ever," I answered; "what do you propose to do later on?"

"That is what we've got to find out," he replied. "In the meantime we must keep him up like this, and take it in turns to watch him. You had better go out now and get a breath of fresh air. If you see your sweetheart, pacify her with the best excuse you can think of."

"Are you quite sure you are safe with him alone?" I asked.

"I must risk it," he replied. But as I moved towards the door, he stopped me.

"Ingleby," he said, speaking slowly and sadly, "I don't know whether you will believe me or not when I say how deeply I regret what has happened in this case. I would have given anything, my own life even, that things should not have fallen out in this way. And what is more, I do not say this for my own sake."

"You are thinking of Consuelo," I said.

"I am," he answered. "It is for her sake I feel the regret. As a rule, I am not given to sentiment, but somehow this seems altogether different. But there, go away and tell her what you think best."

I left him and went in search of Consuelo. She was in her usual place in the tower above her room. And when she saw me she ran to greet me with outstretched hands. Something—it might have been my pale face—frightened her.

"My darling," I said, "you are not ill, are you? What makes you look so alarmed?"

"I have been frightened," she answered; "more frightened than I can tell you."

For a moment I thought she must have heard about her great-grandfather, but such was not the case.

"I have only been up here a few moments," she answered. "The caretaker's wife was in my room when I left. The door was open, and, as I climbed the turret stairs, I thought I heard her call me. Turning round, I was about to descend again, when I saw, standing at the foot of the stairs, a man. He was looking up at me. For a moment I could scarcely believe my eyes. Who do you think it was?"

Though I could easily guess, I managed to force myself to utter the word "Who?"

"He was the man you saw behind the rock, the same I saw bending over me in my cabin on board the *Dona Mercedes*, that terrible Chinaman with half an ear."

I feared that she might see from my face that I knew more than I cared to tell; but, as good fortune had it, she failed to notice it.

"Surely you must have been mistaken," I answered. "What could the man be doing in the castle?"

"She ran to greet me with outstretched hands."

"I do not know," she answered. "But I am as certain I saw him as I am of anything. He was standing at the foot of the stairs, watching me. Then he began to move in my direction; but before he could reach the bottom step, I heard a door open along the corridor. This must have frightened him, for he fled round the corner, and I saw no more of him."

"It must have been my opening the door that saved you," I said. "Thank God I came when I did!"

"But what does it mean?" she asked. "Why did that man come on board the boat, and why has he followed us here?"

"I think the reason is to be found in the fact that he is Dr. Nikola's enemy," I replied. "They had a private quarrel in China some years ago, and ever since then this man has been following him about the world, endeavouring to do him harm. The case is a serious one, darling, and as you love me you must run no risks. Be on your guard night and day. See that your door is locked at night, and never venture from your room after dusk, unless I am with you. It makes my blood run cold when I think of your running such risks as you did this morning."

"But what about you?" she said, looking up at me with her beautiful, frightened eyes. "Oh, why cannot we take my grandfather and go away, and never see this dreadful place again?"

"We must wait patiently," I answered; "the Don is not fit to travel just yet."

She gave a little sigh, and next moment it was time for me to leave her.

For the next two or three days following, Nikola and I took it in turns to act as sentry over the Don. If it was not difficult work, it was the reverse of pleasant; for as soon as the effect of each successive opiate wore off, his evil nature invariably reasserted itself. Sometimes he would sit for an hour or more watching me, as if he intended springing upon me the instant I was off my guard. At others he would crouch in a corner, tearing into atoms everything within his reach. More than once he was really violent, and it became necessary for me to signal to Nikola for assistance. The horror of those days I shall never forget. When I say that, not once but several times, I have left that room dripping with perspiration, the pure sweat of terror, my feelings may be partially imagined. It was not madness we had to contend with; it was worse than that. It was the fighting of a lost soul against the effect of man's prying into what should have been the realms of the unknowable.

"This sort of thing cannot last much longer," said Nikola, when our patient was lying drugged and helpless upon his mattress on the third night after the death of Ah-Win. And I knew he was right. Outraged nature would avenge herself.

When Nikola had bade me good-night, I examined the Don to make sure that he was not shamming sleep in order to try and get the better of me directly I was alone. Finding him to be quite helpless, I seated myself in my chair and prepared to spend my watch in as comfortable a fashion as possible under the circumstances. During the day I had passed a considerable portion of my time with my sweetheart in the open air, and, in consequence, I found myself growing exceedingly sleepy. Knowing it would never do to allow slumber to get the better of me in that room, I rose from my chair and began to pace the floor. This had the effect of temporarily rousing me, and, when I reseated myself, I thought I had dispelled the attack. It soon returned, however, and this time it would not be denied. I rubbed my eyes, I pinched myself, I got up and walked about. It was no good, however, I returned to my chair, my eyelids closed, and, almost without knowing it, I dozed off. When I woke again, it was with a start. I rubbed my eyes and looked about me. Heavens! what mischief had I done? *The Don was not in his corner, the key was gone from the hook upon which it usually hung, and, worse than all, the door stood open!*

For a moment I was so overwhelmed with horror that I could do nothing. But only for a moment. Then I knew that I must act, and at once. I rang the bell for Nikola, and, having done so, dashed into the hall. Almost simultaneously Nikola made his appearance, coming from his room.

"What is the matter?" he cried. "Why do you ring for me?"

"The Don has escaped!" I almost shouted. "Like the fool I am, I fell asleep, and during that time he must have recovered his wits, stolen the key, and escaped from the room. Oh, what have I done? If she should see him as he is, it will kill her!"

For a moment it looked as if Nikola would have swept me off the face of the earth, but the look scarcely came into his eyes before it was gone again.

"We must find him," he cried, "before he can do any mischief, and, what is more, we must not separate, for he would be more than a match for us single-handed."

Accordingly we left the hall and proceeded towards the Dona Consuelo's apartments. I thanked Heaven when I found that the door was locked. Calling to her, in answer to her cry of "Who is there?" I told her that I only desired to assure myself of her safety, and after that we passed on up the turret stairs and along the battlements, but no sign of the Don could we discover there. Returning to the corridor again, we descended to the great entrance hall and searched the courtyard and basement.

The moon shone clear, and the courtyard was as light as day. Had there been any one there, we must certainly have seen him. Suddenly there rang out the most unearthly scream it has ever been my ill-luck to hear. It came from the direction of the chapel, which lay between the keep and what had once been the banqueting hall. From where we stood the interior of the latter was quite visible to us. On either side it had tall windows, so that the light shone directly through. The scream had scarcely died away before we distinctly saw a short figure dash into the room, and out again upon the other side. An instant later and a taller figure followed, and also disappeared. Again and again the scream rang out, while Nikola stood rooted to the spot, unable to move hand or foot.

"I see it all!" cried Nikola. "That was Quong Ma and the other was the Don. They'll kill each other if they meet."

I thought of Consuelo, and of the terror she would feel should she hear that dreadful noise.

"They must not meet!" I cried. "It is too terrible. At any cost we must prevent it Where do you think they are now?"

As if to let us know, another scream rang out. This time it came from our own quarters.

"Come on!" cried Nikola, and dashed into the building. As you may suppose, I followed close upon his heels. In this order we flew up the stairs and along the first gallery, intending, if possible, to reach the small hall by the staircase near the kitchen in which Ah-Win had worked, and thus cut them off. As we crossed the threshold however, a wild hubbub came from the passage ahead, and told us that we were too late. I knew what it meant, and, if I had not been by that time quite bankrupt of emotions, I should certainly have been doubly terrified now.

Leaving the kitchen, we dashed along the passage, only to find that the room usually occupied by Nikola's unfortunates was empty. With the exception of one solitary specimen, who by reason of his infirmity was unable to fly, they had all vanished. Leaving him to his own desires, we passed the iron gate, now thrown open, and a moment later had entered the hall itself. Once more the cry sounded, this time coming from a spot somewhat nearer Consuelo's apartment. On hearing it, my heart seemed to stand still. What if she should imagine that I was in danger and should open her door? The same thought must have been in Nikola's mind, for I heard him say to himself—"Anything but that."

"Again and again the scream rang out."

Side by side we raced for her door, only to find it was still shut and locked.

Almost at the same instant a scream, louder than any we had yet heard, sounded from the battlements above.

"At last!" I cried, and led the way up the stone stairs. I can only say that of all the horrid scenes I have ever witnessed, that I saw before me then was the very worst. In the centre of the open space between the parapets, fighting like wild beasts, were the two men of whom we were in search. Their arms were twined about each other, and, as they swayed to and fro, the sound of their heavy breathing could be distinctly heard. Having reached the top of the stairs, we paused irresolute. What was to be done? To have attempted to separate them would only have been to draw their anger upon ourselves, and to have made the fight a general one. The moon shone down upon us, revealing the smooth sea on one side and the many turrets of the castle on the other. From fighting in the centre of the open space, they gradually came nearer the parapet of the wall. Quong Ma must then have realised how near he stood to death, for he redoubled his energy.

"They will be over!" shouted Nikola, and started to run towards them. He had scarcely spoken before they reached the edge. For a moment, locked in each other's arms, they paused upon the brink; then, with a wild shriek from Quong Ma, they lost their balance and disappeared. I clapped my hands to my eyes to shut out the fearful sight. When I took them away again, all was over, and both Nikola and I knew that Quong Ma and Don Miguel de Moreno were dead.

I suppose I must have fainted, for when I returned to my senses once more, I found myself seated on the top of the stairs, and Consuelo's arms about me.

There remains but little more to tell.

At the time of that dreadful scene upon the battlements it was full tide; and though Nikola and I searched every nook and cranny along the coast-line for many miles, the bodies of the two men could not be found. In all probability they had drifted out to sea. The same day I summoned up my courage, and prepared to tell my sweetheart everything; but when I sought her out, and was about to commence my confession, she stopped me.

"Say nothing to me about it, dear," she began. "I cannot bear it yet. Dr. Nikola has told me everything. He exonerates you completely."

"But what of ourselves?" I asked. "Consuelo, you and I are alone together in the world; will you give me the right to care for your future happiness? My darling, will you be my wife?"

"When and where you please," she answered, holding out her hands to me and looking up at me with her beautiful, trusting eyes. I told her of my straitened means, and how hard the struggle would be at first.

"No matter," she answered bravely, "we will fight the world together. I am used to poverty, and with you beside me I shall know no fear."

A hour later I had an interview with Nikola in the hall.

"Ingleby," he said, "this *is* the end of our intercourse. I have tried my experiment, and though I have succeeded in many particulars, I have failed in the main essential. How much I regret what has happened, I must leave you to imagine; but it is too late—what is done cannot be undone. I have given orders that the yacht shall be prepared. She will convey you to Newcastle, whence you can proceed in any direction you may desire. One thing is certain: Dona Consuelo must leave this place, and, as you are to be her husband, it is only fit and proper that you should go with her. I have only one wish to offer you: it is that you may be as happy as these past weeks have been sad."

He held out his hand to me, and I took it.

"We shall meet no more," he said. "Go away and forget that you ever met Dr. Nikola. Goodbye."

"Goodbye," I answered. Without another word he turned and left the room.

Shortly before midday we boarded the yacht. Steam was up when we arrived, and within a few minutes we were steaming out of the little bay. Consuelo and I stood together at the taffrail, and looked up at the grim old castle on the cliff above our heads. Standing on the battlements we could distinctly see a solitary figure, who waved his hands to us. Then the little vessel passed round the headland, and that was the last we saw of Dr. Nikola.

THE END

Printed in the United Kingdom by
Lightning Source UK Ltd., Milton Keynes
141495UK00001B/255/P